THE COSMIC KINGS

By
EDMOND HAMILTON

I0616967

ARMCHAIR FICTION
PO Box 4369, Medford, Oregon 97504

FORSAKING ALL FOR UNLIMITED ACCESS TO THE COSMOS!

One crewmate was dead, the other seriously injured, and a ruthless enemy had quickly surrounded their ship—Bryant could only think of one place to run to and hide—the "abandoned" planet of Midway!
But on Midway, the subterranean city he remembered from his youth was not as it once had been. Something was amiss. Complicating matters even further was the sudden appearance of their brutal alien pursuers. Soon his beloved city was being plundered by the enemy!

With the realization that the planet wasn't uninhabited after all, Bryant knew he had to risk all—perhaps even his own life—to warn the natives of the danger he had brought to their world. But would they heed his call to action, or were they so certain that they were as powerful as Cosmic Kings?

FOR A COMPLETE SECOND NOVEL, TURN TO PAGE 89

CAST OF CHARACTERS

HUGH BRYANT

A tough space pilot on a top-secret mission, vital to the security of the Rim, unfortunately for him the enemy caught on.

JIM FELTRIE

An inter-galactic intel-man, Feltrie was wanted for the information he carried on microfilm—and in his head.

GRACH CHAI

This brutal Varkonid Commander was a relentless hunter, and unafraid to cut a path of destruction to catch his prey!

PHAON

He fled from home with his children, only to learn he must sacrifice all to save those who would kill them.

BELATH

This hardened fighter had a soft spot for his sister and would do anything—and kill anyone—to protect her.

CYRA

Deemed a forbidden child by the Council, she was raised in secrecy and returning home might well mean her demise.

THE COUNCIL

This all-powerful assembly determined how many children a couple could bear—and law breakers faced the House of Sleep!

CHAPTER ONE

SITTING HUNCHED and dazed with weariness at the controls of the racing scout-ship, Hugh Bryant looked down at the thing in his hand. His lucky piece, which he'd carried since boyhood.

"And fine luck it's brought me," he thought bitterly. *"All the years, and now it all ends like this…"*

The scout-ship was in overdrive, but the compensator screens of the scanning device showed a visual image of space around it. On both flanks, there was nothing. Behind, the Greater Magellanic Cloud hung like a curtain of misty radiance against the inter-galactic emptiness. Ahead, seen edge on, the Rim of the galaxy clove the darkness like a flaming sword.

Bryant sat, fingering the lucky piece, trying to think. But his mind was too tired. He could hardly remember whether they were in overdrive or not. He had forgotten whether Feltrie, in the narrow bunk behind him, was dead or only asleep. He could only remember the huge fact of the pursuers behind them.

Behind them? No, all around them now. The ultrascope showed little red pips in a three-dimensional pattern around the scout. The pips were Varkonid fast raiders, under the command of a particular Varkonid named Grach Chai. The pips were death, closing in very fast and sure.

He wished he'd never heard of Grach Chai, or Varkon, or this doomed mission. He wanted to forget all the years of toil and danger out here on the frontier of the galaxy. He wished he were a boy again, back in the magic place where he had found this lucky piece. Back in the city that was all his own.

"The city," Bryant thought. *"My city. If only I'd never left it. If only I could have stayed."*

On the ultra-scope globe the red pips moved swiftly, closing in. The warning note sounded continuously. The vast wheel-edge of the galaxy blazed in incredible splendor. Feltrie—at this moment probably the most important man on the whole star-frontier—slept, or died, in the narrow bunk. Bryant dreamed.

Twenty-one years ago, and yet he remembered his city clearly. He had been very young then. His family had left that world of the red star when he was only fourteen, when the spaceport had to be abandoned because Varkonid raids had brought trade to a standstill in that whole sector of the Rim.

Bryant tried to remember how it had felt to be young, but he could not. He could only remember the wonderful place that he alone had found on that world. The buried city that no one else knew existed, the magic refuge where he could escape the restrictions of the spaceport colony and the watchfulness of parents. Down in that hidden city that belonged only to him, he had lived. It had been his real world. The other was only something to be endured.

He remembered how he had hated to leave that world. How he had gone down into his city for the last time, how he had wandered through the streets, touching the walls, listening to the hushed echoes of his steps, looking at all the beautiful things he would have to leave behind. And how the sound of his own voice had echoed back to him in bits like broken silver when he cried, "I won't go! I won't!"

But all the time he had known that it was no use, because there was no food here, and finally he had had to get up and go out of the city, taking only one small thing from it with him.

He had it in his hand now—his lucky piece; A bit of curved crystal set on a round metal back, and encircled by a tubular frame of the same white metal. A meaningless, useless thing—but a reminder of the lost magic of his city.

Bryant looked at it, dreaming. The warning note from the ultrascope sounded louder and louder, and he gave no heed. Of a sudden, the pursuers did not matter.

For as he looked at the soft clear spot of light in his palm, his mind, emptied and purified by exhaustion, saw the solution to its problem as a thing of sublime simplicity.

"The city," he whispered. "I was safe there, from everybody. I'll go back there."

He would take Feltrie to the city and keep him there until Grach Chai and the Varkonides quit looking for him.

It was as easy as that.

BLINKING his red-rimmed eyes, Bryant began to concentrate on procedure. He missed Wallace, his co-pilot, astrogator, and sidekick on this half-witted mission, but Wallace was dead. Definitely dead, and his body was back on Varkon. Bryant was going to have to do this by himself.

The first thing was to feed the chart-designation numbers of the red star into the calc machine. He did this, being pretty sure that he remembered them right. While he waited for the coordinates he looked at the red pips on the telltale globe. The Varkonid ships had him completely caged.

Well, let them. He had his lucky piece. He had his place to go. He was unstoppable.

With a sort of low animal cunning, he regarded the speeding pips, and laughed.

The tape rattled out of the calc machine, neatly punched for a new course. He left it there for the moment, and counted carefully on his outspread fingers the several steps of what he had decided to do, pointing each time with the other hand to the correlated object—overdrive master-control, normal manual operational control, tape, main bank scanner slot, overdrive master-control.

One. Two. Three. Four. Five.

He turned to the ultrascope globe, put his thumb to his nose, and waggled his fingers at the red pips.

Then he did Step One, slamming the master-control bar from Positive to Negative.

Automatic relays took the ship out of overdrive and into normal space, and that was as well, because Bryant passed out. There were ways to cushion the shock of translation, but Bryant had not bothered with them. When he could focus his fuzzy sight again the scout was moving along in open space at a speed which, relative to its previous velocity in stellar overdrive, was like standing still.

Bryant began normal operating procedure. Step Two.

Feltrie groaned. He was a small lean, man who looked like an amiable ferret. His head had been shaved to allow for a Varkonid disguise, and the hair was now growing back in, spiky and grizzled. He struggled up and sat on the edge of the bunk.

"What the hell are you trying to do?" he demanded. A sprayed-on plastic dressing on the side of his head showed the edges of a new wound. He held this tenderly with one hand and groaned again. "Kill me?" he added, as an afterthought.

Bryant pointed to the radar screen. "Look there."

Faint objects were appearing in a globular pattern, far ahead.

"They've run right over us. See?" He illustrated, holding one hand still in mid-air and passing the other over it very fast, making a whistling sound through his teeth. Feltrie looked at him closely.

"Are you okay?" he asked.

"I'm fine," said Bryant. "Don't confuse me." He counted on his fingers again. Tape. Main bank scanner slot. Steps Three and Four.

He did them, placing the tape in the slot and listening to the subdued clatter of relays setting up the new course.

"Hang on," Bryant said.

Rockets fired in precise succession. The scout flipped over at a right angle to its former direction. Feltrie came out of the bunk and skidded into the bulkhead, where he stayed. Bryant looked at his thumb, nodded, and threw the overdrive master from Negative back to Positive.

Step Five.

The Varkonides would come after him again, Bryant knew. Even a brilliant piece of strategy like this trick he had just played would not throw them off forever, especially not with Grach Chai in command. But they might be delayed enough so that the scout could reach the misty galactic arm toward which it was now headed, and which would have enough stellar debris to confuse the Varkonid ultrascopes at least temporarily. With enough luck, he might even reach Midway, the world of the red star, and get clear out of space before they could pick him up again.

Once on Midway, in his own beautiful city, he would be safe. Nobody could find him there. Ever.

Smiling grimly, Bryant sagged gratefully into oblivion. At the very last a twinge of doubt crossed his face and he tried to open his eyes again, but it was far too late.

The scout, on autopilot, raced for the out-flung spiral arm in which an old red star drifted on its endless journey around the Rim of the Milky Way.

CHAPTER TWO

SEEN AGAIN after a hiatus of twenty-one years, and without the roseate vision of extreme youth, the world of the red star was not much. It had not changed physically in any way. But it had stopped being home, and with a place like this it had to be home to you or you couldn't stand it.

Bryant and Feltrie crouched on the eminence of a low ridge and peered through the crimson dusk of noon at the landscape ahead. Feltrie grunted.

"Well," he said, "I guess it's better than that, anyway."

"Better than that what?" asked Bryant.

"Better than being taken back to Varkon." He shivered, trying to zip his thermo-coverall tighter at the neck. "But not much."

"Okay, okay," said Bryant crossly. "Go on back to the ship and give 'em a call if you want to. But leave me out of it."

Doubt was gnawing at him with increasing force. So he said truculently, "I'll be down in my city safe and sound, sleeping on a golden bed. I'll feel sorry for you."

Feltrie didn't answer that. He only said, "Hadn't we better get going?"

Bryant glanced back into the cliff-locked valley below and far behind them. He had hidden the scout as well as he could there, but anyone who was really looking for it could probably find it. He might have put it into one of the hangars of the old spaceport, which he had passed over coming in, and which were only partly buried and at least partly intact. But if the Varkonides did come, that would be the first place they would look.

He squinted anxiously at the murky sky, with stars showing against the midday glare of the dying sun. He did not see any ships, but he was not nearly so convinced of the brilliance of his plan as he had been when he thought it up.

He had landed the scout only a short while before sundown, and since nothing that lived could survive a night in the open here, unprotected, they had stayed in the ship until the next morning, a period of forty-three hours by the chronometer. At interstellar velocities, that was a lot of time in which to be caught up to, and his ultrascope was of course inoperative now, so he had no way to check.

Feltrie was right. They had better get going.

They had had to waste some time waiting for the air to get warm enough to breathe, and then it had taken them the rest of the long morning to climb the ridge. Midway was big and the gravity was heavier than they were used to on their home worlds, and they were loaded with every ounce of rations they could carry.

"There's water in the city," Bryant had said. "Plenty of it."

Or there had been, twenty-one years ago.

Feltrie had insisted on carrying all they could, anyway, which wasn't much. Enough to last them three days if they were careful. But it was heavy, too.

They started down the slope of the ridge, toward the great plain that spread as far as they could see north, south, and west of the worn-down mountain chain, which was no more now than a series of naked humps of rock. The plain was the color of old rust. If you watched it you could see it move, creeping and crawling sluggishly where the cold wind pushed it. When you walked on it your boots sank over the ankle with every step, and when you pulled them out the dust rolled back into the hollow and there was no sign that you had ever passed that way.

"Is it all like this?" asked Feltrie.

"Pretty much. There's a few other low stumps of old mountains here and there, but most of it's like this—drowned in its own dust."

There was only one landmark. The tall signal pylon, the drifted domes and installations of the spaceport, abandoned these twenty-one years to the cold and the dark and the bitter winds.

"I suppose," said Feltrie, "that there was an excellent reason for having a spaceport here?" He was a Middle Sector man, and not familiar with this part of the Rim.

Bryant said, "The best. It's a halfway point, or was, for four main routes of galactic trade. This area of space is not overcrowded with stars, and this happens to be the most conveniently located system with a habitable planet."

They skidded and stumbled together down a long chute filled with rubble and rotten stones. The red dust rose up behind them in a heavy cloud.

"Habitable," repeated Feltrie. He pulled the hood of his coverall down until he could hardly see out from under it. "I suppose it's all in how you define the word."

"The air isn't poisonous, the gravity isn't crushing, and under domes you can live very comfortably." Bryant's tone was sharp, but his gaze was abstracted, turning more and more often toward the sky. The red sun hung huge and listless, and the cold stars glimmered in a void the color of blue ink.

"Listen," he said suddenly, "if anything happens and we get separated, remember the entrance is exactly northeast of the pylon two and one quarter miles. Got that?"

"Got it. But what…"

"It may be buried, but not far. The surface level had stabilized when the last section was added on. Scratch around till you find it."

He had done this so often as a child that it did not seem in the least ambiguous. But Feltrie looked at him and said,

"We just better not get separated."

THEY REACHED the bottom of the slope. Their boots sank in the yielding dust. They began to walk heavily across the plain. From time to time Feltrie put his gloved hand against the front of his coverall jacket and felt the small bulge inside that was made by the case of microfilm spools for which all this was being done.

Bryant continued to look often at the sky.

The red sun sagged over into afternoon. Their shadows, black on red, lengthened behind them. The hollows the wind had made in the dust began to show pools of darkness in their deep places and bars of crimson light on their western crests. The men were tired, but the spaceport and the tall Pylon were now only three miles or so away.

In the end it was Feltrie who saw them coming after all. Bryant was studying his compass and trying to figure distance from the pylon, and Feltrie said, "Get down!" in a voice like a pistol shot.

Bryant got down. Flat. Feltrie dropped beside him. They lay motionless, except that Bryant turned his head so that he could see.

Two Varkonid cruisers were coming in, still high up and far away, catching the red light on their hulls.

"Think they saw us?"

"Hardly, at that distance."

Two men, tiny motes on a creeping desert. Infinitesimal. Invisible. Bryant burrowed deeper into the dust. He felt as big as a mountain, and as naked.

"If we lie still," said Feltrie, "I don't think they'll spot us."

They lay still.

Over the mountains the two cruisers separated and one swung north along the line of cliffs where they joined the desert. The other one came on.

"Heading for the spaceport," said Bryant. "I told you."

"That other one's liable to find our ship, anyway."

"But they'll expect to find us near it. If there's no sign of us around the spaceport, they'll start combing the hills."

"Unless they know about the city."

"Nobody," said Bryant, "knows about that but me."

"Okay," said Feltrie. "But you've got to admit it seems almost impossible, a find of that magnitude…"

"What does a kid eleven years old know about things like that? I stumbled on it, literally. I found it, it was mine, and I never told anybody."

"Why?"

"Because," said Bryant simply, "I knew they wouldn't let me keep it."

The second cruiser went ripping over their heads and made a landing, in booming thunder and bursting flame, on the drifted but still solid tarmac of the port. Bryant smiled in spite of himself. You had to hand it to the old man. His father might have been emotionally dense, mentally inflexible, and shamefully henpecked, but he could build spaceports. He had built this one and kept it operative, and even after two decades of neglect it was still sound.

The cruiser squatted like a dark tower against the west. Bryant recognized it as the command ship. Grach Chai's own. Small black figures came out of it and spread quickly among the various domes.

The wind blew stronger. The red dust rolled over the two men, blending their drab coveralls more closely into the landscape. Bryant began to feel the cold in spite of his heated suit. After a while he began to shiver.

"Won't the so-and-so ever go?" snarled Feltrie through chattering teeth. He was referring to Grach Chai.

"He's thorough," Bryant said.

"Very thorough."

"Suppose they decide to stay there?"

"Why should they?" Bryant snapped. But he peered at the sun, growing redder and more enormous as it sank. The dust blew into his eyes and gritted in his mouth. He began to calculate the exact distance and direction to the city entrance from the pylon. They would not have any margin for mistakes. They would have to find it pretty quickly on the first try, or not at all.

THE DARK FIGURES moved busily through the extensive installations of the port. Bryant watched them with a bitter and active hatred. Anti-social elements like the Varkonides might be possible these days only in the frontier sectors along the Rim, but no matter how archaic and improbable they might seem to Inner Sector dwellers and the extremely distant Galactic Council, they were a constant, daily, and painfully real threat to the people of the Rim.

You couldn't call the Varkonides pirates, because they were a homogenous race and culture, and acts of violence against the property of other peoples was a part of their culture-pattern and a command of their religion.

You couldn't call them a warlike aggressor and whistle up the forces of the United Navy to deal with them, either, because they did not attack in large bodies, nor with any idea of conquest.

They were masters of the hit-and-run raid. Some fool in the forgotten past had taught them how to build spaceships, and they had taken to space like young eagles to the air. They had had a perfectly beautiful time of it until the advancing tide of Civilization began to make them trouble.

Seventy years or so ago they had run head on into a Frontier Civilian Defense Committee, operating with no official sanction but with a great anger, and the Varkonides had been driven right off their home planet of Varkon, and right off the edge of the galaxy. In a few decades people had forgotten all about them, and trade flourished along the Rim. Then, from a new Varkon somewhere in the Magellanic Cloud, the Varkonides had come forth refreshed and strengthened, to prey like happy wolves on the haunts of men. Grach Chai was one of their most noted captains, and Bryant had brushed with him before.

Bryant wondered what Feltrie must be thinking, lying there with those micro-films clutched to his chest. With Bryant and the late Bud Wallace to do the flying, he had spent months in the island archipelago of stars, looking for Varkon. When it was found he had actually landed there and taken pictures of the defenses. The current Frontier Committee had paid Feltrie a very large sum to do this, and now they would have enough dope on the Varkonides to give them another decisive lesson—perhaps drive them out of the Cloud and right on to Andromeda—if they ever got the films and the additional information stored in Feltrie's battered head.

Bryant guessed that he was probably thinking what the Varkonides would do to him if they got him back. And he was probably thinking that they would not rest until they did get him back. They couldn't afford to. Not if they wanted to go on living on the fat of the Rim without ever getting hit back. Not if they wanted to go on living, period.

The rim of the sun touched the horizon. It had become dreadfully cold. The air was perfectly dry. It cut like a sharp knife into nose and throat and lungs. Bryant wept with the pain of it, and the tears froze on his dusty cheeks.

The Varkonid search-parties began to return to their ship.

In an agony of cold and impatience, the two men waited.

The cruiser took off, in a roll of thunder and a flash of flame. It headed north toward the mountains.

The men rose stiffly and began to run.

The sun sank lower and the light died. Bryant tried to watch the pylon, almost indistinguishable now in the hazy redness, and the compass in his hand all at the same time. He was very tired and very cold. He was afraid. The darkling plain spread whispering around him, infinite and sad. He did not think he would be able to find one particular point in it, without light or time to search.

Feltrie was not asking any questions now. It was as though he did not want to hear the answers.

Blinking, straining his vision against the wind and the last dusk, Bryant made one final sighting on the pylon and put his compass away.

"It ought to be here," he said. They looked at the blowing dust, at their feet that seemed to be wading in dark blood.

Nothing.

"Spread out a little bit," said Bryant. "Look for it. Dig!"

They scrabbled and scrambled on all fours like two shambling dogs, pawing in the dust.

The sun sank. The last vague afterglow vanished. The plain turned black and the stars burned like diamonds in the sky, scattered and remote. It was night.

Bryant's freezing hands felt something solid underneath the dust.

"Here," he said. "Here it is. Dig."

They scooped the dust away, flinging it wildly into the black wind.

"That's enough," Bryant panted. "Here. They set these all around in a ring so you could find them easy…"

He pressed down hard on a raised bar. The blackness stirred.

There was sound, dim and muffled.

There was light.

A round section of metal lifted up from the plain, showering dust off its edges. A puff of warm air blew across Bryant's face. He looked at Feltrie in the soft white light and laughed and hugged him tight around the shoulders.

"Come on," he said. "Come on in."

They stepped under the metal section. There was a floor, also of metal, and a thick central column with a control board on it.

"It works just like an elevator," Bryant said. "See?"

He pressed the small bar of the control, and the floor sank gently down a metal-walled shaft. The roof section dropped into place above them, shutting out the bitter night. Into warmth and brilliance they fell, into a chamber with unadorned walls and a single door.

Bryant took his lucky piece out of his pocket and kissed it.

"Didn't I tell you?" he said. He was laughing. "Didn't I? See, it's all right. We're home."

He flung open the door.

CHAPTER THREE

ALMOST INSTANTLY some center of sensitivity in Bryant told him that something was wrong.

And yet there was nothing he could see.

He stood just beyond the doorway, with Feltrie beside him, and that in itself was strange, because he had never before come through that door except alone. Suddenly he resented Feltrie, and he decided that that was the trouble. Nobody else had any business here. This was his place, and his alone.

That was a ridiculous attitude to take, he realized, after all the trouble he had gone through to get Feltrie here. And the idea had been exclusively his own. But Bryant was tired with a long exhaustion and a long fear. His nerves were pulled to the snapping point. His grasp on time and reality and common sense were highly unstable. He resented Feltrie. He couldn't help it.

The moment of return should have been his, all alone.

He walked slowly across the little circular court, paved in blue, to the gate of white metal wrought in a simple grille. The gate was open. No other hand should have touched it in the twenty-one years since he had passed through it for the last time. He tried to remember if he had left it open, but he could not.

Feltrie followed him through the gate, keeping behind Bryant, walking softly and not speaking. Bryant had talked quite a lot about the city during moments aboard the scout. Feltrie was a tactful man, and a reasonably wise one. He understood that the city was to Bryant everything that he had lacked in his boyhood, the playmate and companion, the wonder and the dream. He let Bryant have his reunion as undisturbed as possible. But he kept close to him, and his eyes, inflamed with dust, peered watchfully, as full of suspicion as they were with amazement.

Beyond the gate a long straight avenue led between rows of buildings toward a distant plaza. The buildings were not high, three and four stories at the most. They appeared, from their mellow covering and the softened outlines of their ornamental carvings, to be extremely old. From the weathered look of the stone, they had already been old when the protective dome replaced the sky, shutting out wind and rain and frost forever.

The dome made a low vault overhead, no more than fifty feet above the highest buildings. The red dust covered it. Neither man knew by how much, but it was obviously deep, judging from how far they had dropped from the surface. To

Bryant it was just the way it had always been. To Feltrie it was claustrophobic. He flinched from the thought of it. Almost in panic he looked at the thick supports that marched in file like soldiers behind the rows of houses.

They seemed solid enough. So did the plates of metal or plastic that formed the dome. He was only a little comforted.

The pavement of the avenue was a pleasant yellow. There were four main avenues in the city, dividing it exactly into four sections, and each avenue was a different color. The houses were not all of stone—some were of plastics or cement. They showed soft shades of rose and gold, green, blue, every color that was pleasing to the eye. Vines clambered over some of them, and shrubs and flowers grew in plots of ground watered from a hidden source underneath. But they grew rankly, choked, neglected.

Feltrie sniffed the warm, fresh air. Obviously there was a central refresher plant and pumping station. The light, which approximated that of a Sol-type star, came from a webwork of tubes that arched across the dome. It would, theoretically, contain all the normal sunlight components.

Walking behind Bryant on the yellow avenue, Feltrie had to admit that the city was beautiful. But he hated it. He hated the lowering dome, frail shield against a horrid death. He hated the silence. There was too much of it, a whole city full of it, intense and unbroken, so that the sound of their footsteps and their breathing was like the shouting of a crowd.

Bryant's face remained rapt and joyful. His gaze moved here and there, welcoming old landmarks and memories. But gradually, as he neared the oval plaza in which the four main avenues met, a puzzled shadow began to creep into his eyes.

The buildings that fronted the plaza were all white, severely simple in line and imposing in spite of their low elevation. A line of carved memorial stelae bisected the length of the oval. They too were white, and the effect of all this whiteness after the colored streets was stunning. As Feltrie moved closer to the stelae, he saw that there were human-like figures carved on them as well as text.

BRYANT LAID his hand on the first stela and looked around at the white buildings in the stillness. For the first time he spoke.

"It's just the same," he said, "and yet it isn't."

"Twenty-one years is a long time," Feltrie said.

Bryant looked around him slowly, wondering and sad. "It's just a city," he said. "It's not..." He hesitated, searching for a word. "It's not *mine* any more."

He felt a terrible sense of loss, that he could not understand.

Feltrie put it into words. "You were fourteen then. Now you're thirty-five."

Bryant frowned. He shook his head again, and looked down at the bit of shining crystal he still held in his hand. His lucky piece, the talisman that recalled the dream. He put it down on the stone beside him and sat miserably with his head hanging.

Feltrie said gently, "Hadn't we better find a place to sleep? I don't know about you, but I'm bushed."

Bryant sighed and got up. "Take your pick. Any house. They're all furnished. When the people left this place they didn't take anything but their personal belongings."

"Where did they go?" asked Feltrie. "And why? They sure left everything as though they intended to come back."

Bryant said irritably, "How should I know?"

He started off toward the mouth of the avenue that was paved in red. There was a particular house on the opposite, apple-green avenue, but he did not have the heart to go there now. That had been the core of the dream, his own house where he was master. He had brought things to it from all over the city, things that pleased him, to be placed and used as he wanted them, with no one to question or deny. Kid stuff, he thought. Feltrie's right. I'm older now. Old. That's all.

They chose a turquoise-colored house near the plaza. It was pleasant and spacious inside, the interior surfaces done in pastel shades. There were metal jalousies at the windows to provide privacy. The sleeping chambers had solid shutters to provide night in a place of endless day. The furniture was simple, highly stylized, and quite beautiful. Everything was there except the personal things. There was no dust. It was as though the people who belonged there had just stepped out and would return. Feltrie was almost reluctant to appropriate one of the beds.

Water still ran in the conduits. Bryant had drunk it many times before without ill effect, so they used it lavishly. They ate some of their rations and then talked briefly, before they turned in. Feltrie insisted on standing watch and watch about, and Bryant finally gave in. They flipped a coin, and Feltrie got the first watch.

"Good," said Bryant. "Enjoy yourself." He stretched out on the yielding mattress. He was dog tired. He felt like a child that has just had a terrible disappointment. He wanted to sleep and forget the whole thing.

But Feltrie said, "What happens if the Varkonides find our ship and decide to wait there until we come back?"

Bryant cursed him, "Can't you think of anything good happening? I don't know what happens then. You figure it out, and tell me."

"Oh, by the way," said Feltrie. "I thought you might want this again." He was holding the lucky piece in his hands. "Odd sort of a gadget, isn't it? Look, you can move the metal frame a quarter turn each way."

"I know," said Bryant. "But it doesn't open or anything." He took it and laid it on a low stand beside the bed. "Thanks. I guess I forgot it."

Feltrie sat down in a padded reclining chair, where he could look out the window.

Bryant slept.

He slept heavily, dreamlessly, at the bottom of a quiet well. Then suddenly he was awake, dragged up on a sharp hook of alarm.

Someone was close to him, whispering.

In a sweating quiver of panic, Bryant lay still and listened. There were two people whispering, and neither of them was Feltrie. They were very close to him, so close that it almost seemed he was hearing them inside his head.

Varkonides, Bryant thought. They followed us somehow. We're trapped.

…*strangers,* one of the whisperers was saying. *Not from Kothmar, certainly.*

A second whisperer, excited, forceful. *We must kill them, it's the only way. Now, while they both sleep.*

No. Wait a while. Perhaps…

Wait for what…until they find Cyra?

But they are strangers!

It doesn't matter. Anyone who knows about the city is a danger to us. Let me kill them swiftly, before they wake!

In one wild instinctive movement, Bryant grabbed the gun that lay beside his pillow and sprang half erect, ready to fire.

There was no one in the room.

CHAPTER FOUR

THE CALM and steady light came with the gentle air through the open window. Feltrie, the guard and watcher, slept the sleep of the dead in his chair. The passage beyond the door was deserted. Everything was as they had left it.

The whispering continued, only a little fainter.

Wait. The one on the bed has risen. He's armed. He acts as though he knows...

Impossible, said the other whisperer. *But still, take care, Belath. We don't know what power these strangers may...*

Bryant's gaze fell on the open window. In the pale-gold wall of the neighboring house there was also a window. Its jalousie was partly closed. Bryant thought it had been open when he last saw it, and he thought now that a shadow moved behind it.

He sprang to the wall beside the window, out of sight of the watcher and out of range of a weapon. He reached out and grabbed Feltrie, who woke with a yell. Bryant dragged him away from the window.

"We're being watched," he said. "Be quiet a minute..."

The whispering had stopped.

"Where?" said Feltrie, blinking and dragging out his gun.

"In the next house. I heard them whispering. Come on."

It was not until he was halfway to the front door that Bryant realized the impossibility of what he had just said. But he didn't stop to wonder about it then. He paused, just inside the front door.

Feltrie, awake now, said, "They must have seen us come into the city, in spite of the dark. And if they know we're here, it's only a matter of time. They've got us like mice in a bottle."

"Shhh…" Bryant was listening again. Nothing. The avenue outside was empty. He suddenly turned and ran back to the rear of the house. There was a mews here, running parallel to the front avenue.

Someone disappeared between two houses across the way.

"There! There," said Bryant, "did you see him?"

"Not quite. Just a flicker of motion. But…how did he look to you? Colors, I mean."

Bryant thought carefully. "About the same coloring as me, except the hair was lighter. He looked to be pretty naked except for a little short skirt and something over his shoulder."

Feltrie said, "Wrong color for a Varkonid. I thought so, too."

The Varkonides were a dark olive-green, and the crests they had instead of hair were barred and banded with splendid brilliance. Even at a glimpse you could not mistake them for humans.

The two men looked at each other.

"I thought," said Feltrie, "you said this was a dead city, and that Midway is a dead world."

"It is. They are."

"Then," said Feltrie, "if that wasn't a Varkonid, what was it?"

Bryant shook his head. "I'm damned," he said, "if I know."

Feltrie looked out at the innocent, soundless city. He sighed. "I suppose we'd better start finding out. And it won't be easy."

They went back to the sleeping chamber to get their long-range shock rifles. Bryant was frowning.

"His name was Belath," he said, "and he wanted to kill us. There's something or someone called Cyra that he doesn't want us to find. But the other fellow…"

"What other fellow?" said Feltrie. "What are you talking about?" He looked narrowly at Bryant.

Bryant nodded toward the pale-gold house. "I told you I heard them whispering. Belath was watching us. He was talking to someone else, who wanted him to wait. He said we were strangers." He repeated slowly, "Not from Kothmar, certainly."

"Where is Kothmar?"

Bryant shrugged. "Never heard of it."

Feltrie said, "Come here." He stood by the window and pointed to the window of the opposite house. "Now do you honestly believe you could hear two men whispering over there?"

"No," said Bryant slowly. "And yet I heard them. One of them, the older one…I got the impression he was farther away."

"You were dreaming," said Feltrie.

"I didn't dream the boy we saw."

HE WENT OVER and sat on the bed, feeling tired and confused. Nothing had gone right. There was a curse on him, and on the city. He put on his boots, and zipped them up.

The whispering suddenly began again.

I'm safe, Father. I'm all right, but they knew I was there. I think they saw me. What shall we do now?

I don't know. Come back, and we'll try to plan…

That was all.

"Did you hear it?" cried Bryant, looking around at Feltrie.

"Faintly. But I heard it. Like right here in the room, like right inside my head." Feltrie paused. "Hugh…"

"What?"

"What language were they speaking?"

"English, I guess." Then Bryant said, "No, that's crazy. It must have been Universal, only people don't use that between themselves, in their own families. Why...I don't think they were speaking any language."

"Well," said Feltrie, "telepathy isn't exactly unheard of."

"It is for me," said Bryant. Earth stock, along with a number of other races, had always remained deficient in the esper abilities, no matter how hard they tried. Barring a few individuals, they were just no good at it. Bryant himself was telepathically as dense as a brick wall. He began to feel uncanny, as though someone had practiced witchcraft on him.

He jumped up and slung his rifle over his shoulder. "Let's get out of here," he said, and picked up his lucky piece from the stand by the bed.

The lucky piece was warm. Suddenly, startling as a shout in his ear, Belath's thought-cry echoed in his mind. *"Father, he's found me!"*

"Break contact," said the mind of the other man. *"I'm receiving him too. Break contact!"*

There was a click...whether audible or sensed, Bryant could not tell. There were no more whisperings. He looked at Feltrie, wide-eyed, and Feltrie nodded.

"A quarter-turn either way," he said, "but it doesn't open or do anything. It does something all right, your lucky piece. It's a telepath gadget."

"Nothing ever happened with it before!" said Bryant, staring at the thing he had carried since childhood, and had never understood.

"It never had anyone to talk to before," Feltrie said. "Our friends...Belath and his father...must have these gadgets too. Communicators. Telepathic communicators, like little personal radios, only tuned to the mind, to pick up and boost the electrical impulses of your thought. How well was this world explored?"

Feltrie's zig-zag habit of thinking sometimes got ahead of Bryant. He was still busy with the implications of the communicator, and it was a second or two before the connection became apparent.

"The usual survey was run, I suppose. The planet's one uniform ball of dust, as I told you. No visible signs of any life at all. I don't suppose the surveyors bothered too much. It was so obviously a dead world, and they only wanted to build a spaceport on it. Of course, if the life, the population, was all underground…"

Feltrie finished for him. "They wouldn't have known there was any population…any more than they knew about this city."

Bryant shook his head dazedly. "I just can't believe it. Why wouldn't some of them have contacted *us?* We are here for nearly six years on the surface, building the port, using it…"

"They might not have known about you, if they always live underground. This city was deserted…maybe there isn't another one, an inhabited one, for thousands of miles."

"Then," said Bryant, pointing vaguely in the direction Belath had gone, "how did they get here?"

He looked down at the lucky piece communicator again. Suddenly he began to talk at it, very urgently. "Listen. Listen, don't be afraid of us. We're friends. Friends, understand?" He projected the thought of friendliness as hard as he could.

"No use," said Feltrie, after a minute. "They've shut off their communicators."

"Well," said Bryant, "come on, then. We'll just have to find them the hard way."

They went out into the quiet street, moving cautiously, listening, watching the million blank windows, the corners, the doorways, everything.

They searched, and kept on searching. There was no way of judging time in this place. The light never changed; there was no dusk and no darkness. As a boy, Bryant had loved this feeling of foreverness. Now, searching through the city for someone who wanted earnestly to kill him, it made him feel caught in an unpleasant dream from which he couldn't wake.

They circled around to the other side of the plaza without finding anything. The apple-green avenue was in front of them now, and they could see far down it to where it ended in the circular drive that followed the edge of the dome. Nothing moved.

"Which way now?" said Feltrie.

Bryant shrugged and turned back toward the plaza. "Might as well work back this way."

"You know they can probably stay out of sight as long as they want to."

"Yeah."

They walked slowly back along the avenue, keeping close to the buildings on one side, peering nervously and seeing nothing, straining their ears for a sound and hearing nothing. From time to time Bryant had tried to use the communicator, but there had been no response. Now he said,

"I've got a feeling we're being followed." He moved his shoulders uneasily. "You know what I mean? A cold spot, like someone was watching me."

"I know what you mean."

They went on a little farther.

Bryant put his hand on Feltrie's arm. "I thought I heard something."

They stopped and held their breath. There was nothing. Bryant shuffled his feet loudly, and then held his breath again.

A soft whisper of sound, like the drifting of leaves in a windy night. Only there was no wind.

Bryant spun around and ran between the, houses, with Feltrie at his heels. A curtain of vines hung over the wall of a mist-gray house. At one edge long tendrils swayed and the leaves were shaken.

"Around to the front!" said Bryant in a fierce whisper. Feltrie sped off. Bryant leaped to the wall of the house and flattened himself against it. Then he slid in under the curtain of vines.

There was a doorway, open. He listened. Something moved inside, light and quick, going away. He looked around the edge of the opening. The vines had overgrown the windows and the hall was dim. He saw a shadow in it, at the far end. He stepped inside.

The front door crashed open. Feltrie's rifle appeared, and a cautious segment of Feltrie's head and one shoulder. The shadow stood silhouetted in the sudden light. Bryant's eyes widened, and he shouted to Feltrie, "Hold it! Don't shoot!" He began to run down the hall.

The shadow whirled, stood poised for a single instant, and then rushed toward a doorway at the side of the hall. But Bryant was a little too close. He reached out and grabbed it.

CHAPTER FIVE

IT WAS A VERY solid shadow, lithe, firm, and extremely active. It snarled. It bit and clawed. Bryant kept trying to soothe it, trying to hold it tight and still not hurt it. Feltrie came in and looked at it and grinned.

"I'll be damned," he said.

"Very likely," Bryant panted. "Please," he said, "hold still. I'm not going to hurt you."

He moved toward the open door, toting the shadow with him. It was a girl-shadow, and as the light fell stronger on her all the shadowiness disappeared, leaving just girl. Girl with cream-colored skin and blue-green eyes and hair that would have been dark brown if it hadn't had so much red in it. Girl beautifully formed, quite small, almost fairy-like, and bristling with fear and fury.

"Please," he said. "There now. Take it easy." He smiled.

She tore at him like a little cat.

Bryant said desperately, "What'll I do, Jim? I'm afraid I'm bruising her, but I can't let her go."

Feltrie reached over and said, "Hold her still a minute." She was wearing a chain around her neck, and from it, like a locket, against the breast of the yellow tunic she wore, hung one of the crystal communicators. Feltrie twisted the ring a quarter turn. "Now," he said. "How's that?" He kept his head pushed in close so he could hear too.

Instantly the girl's thought-stream rushed into Bryant's mind, and it was so wild with fear that Bryant was shocked.

"Oh, no," he said. "Please. Listen to me. I wouldn't dream of harming you. Please…"

He poured it on across the tumult of her panic, and gradually a look of doubt came into her eyes and she paused in her clawing.

"You're really not from Kothmar?"

"I don't even know where it is. We're both from other worlds." On a sudden inspiration he said, "We're hiding from enemies, too." He gave her a mental picture of Varkonides, colored by his own feelings into something even more hideous than they were.

She thought that over, looking from him to Feltrie and back again, searching their minds for lies.

"Why did you wish to capture me, then?"

"Just a little while ago someone was planning to kill us while we slept. We were naturally curious to know why. Is Belath by any chance your brother?"

She let her hands drop now. "Yes."

"Hm. And you're Cyra?"

She nodded. "He was only protecting me. We thought at first, of course, that we had been followed, and Belath was determined that I should not be taken back."

"To Kothmar?"

Sadly, she said, "Yes."

Bryant smiled. "And what wicked thing did you do in Kothmar?"

"I'm a Forbidden Child."

Bryant shook his head. "I don't understand."

Feltrie, with his face close to theirs, was looking back along the dim hall. All at once he stiffened and said softly, "Hang onto her, Hugh. Don't let go whatever you do."

Both Bryant and Cyra turned their heads, following the direction of his gaze. A man had come into the hall from one of the adjoining rooms. Probably he had climbed through a window from outside. He was a slight, small man, but his face, in the reflected light from the doorway, was set and determined. He held a weapon in his hands, and it had been Feltrie's idea that as long as they were close to the girl he would not use it.

Cyra cried out to him. She used a quick staccato language that meant nothing to Bryant, but he could follow her thought quite easily through the communicators.

"Father," she was saying. "Wait, they're not enemies…"

THE MAN ANSWERED sharply, one or two words. He moved forward. Then Bryant sensed motion on his other side, and turned, and saw Belath rushing in through the door just behind Feltrie, with something in his hand, upraised and swinging downward. The blow was already started and Bryant couldn't stop it. He could only shout and let go of the girl, and try to pull Feltrie out of the way.

It did not entirely work. The blow was made a glancing one, but on Feltrie's already damaged head it was enough. He turned white and went to his knees. Belath turned on Bryant, his handsome young face drawn out of shape with a kind of frenzy, but Bryant was already moving. He had flung himself headlong over Feltrie, his arms outstretched. They closed on Belath's sinewy waist and bore him over and down.

Cyra's voice sounded with shrill urgency. The man spoke. Bryant and the boy rolled in the doorway, half in, half out. Belath was a tougher proposition than his sister, and Bryant did not want to damage him, either. Out of the corner of his eye, as he thumped and floundered, he saw that the girl had got between them and her father, and that she was talking fast. The man was hesitant, his weapon partly lowered. Feltrie groaned and crawled out of the way of the flailing feet, and sat against the wall holding his head.

Bryant got the boy flattened out and pinioned, smothering him by sheer weight. He looked up panting at the girl.

"Cyra," he said. "Will you tell your brother...?"

"I'll tell him," said the man. He, too, wore a crystal hung around his neck. His manner was still wary, and hardly less grim than it had been. He told the boy to get up and stand quiet. Bryant released his hold, and Belath scrambled sulkily to his feet. His eyes, fixed on Bryant, were resentful and afraid.

Bryant bent over Feltrie, who said weakly that he was all right. Bryant glared at Belath, and said, "You're in an almighty hurry to kill somebody."

"He has a reason," said the man, "as have I." He still carried his weapon so that it could be used at a second's notice. "I am Phaon of Kothmar. Who are you, and what are you doing in Annamar?"

"Annamar," repeated Bryant. "That's the name of the city? I never knew."

Phaon's eyes narrowed. "You've been here before?"

"Many times." He explained, as rapidly as he could, when and how he had been here and why he had returned. "As soon as we can get back to our ship we'll be gone from Midway. We have a vitally important mission to carry out, and it has nothing at all to do with you or Kothmar. So you have no reason to be afraid of us. Matter of fact, it looks for the moment as though we're all fugitives together."

Phaon said, after a minute, "Where is this house you say was yours in time gone by?"

"Right up this avenue, sort of a peach-colored house..." Bryant's thought carried a picture, all bathed in a loving glow, of the house as he had last seen it, the rooms as he had last arranged each treasure. Phaon nodded.

"Very well," he said. "I believe you. We were much puzzled by that house, where the vines had been trimmed from the windows, and the rooms arranged by an alien hand. We could not guess who had been here."

"Your people, living underground, didn't ever know about our surface spaceport years ago?" said Bryant.

"Oh, yes, we knew all about your spaceport, when you came and when you left," said Phaon. "But we didn't know that one of you had been down here in Annamar."

BRYANT WAS STARTLED. "You knew about the spaceport...about us? You came out and spied on us?"

Phaon shrugged. "Kothmar is more than a thousand miles from here, and since our dome was sealed against the engulfing dust we have almost never gone on the surface.

But we could watch you in our own way. We...most of us...were glad when you finally left."

"But why?" exclaimed Bryant. "Why didn't you contact us? You could have emigrated, in our ships, to another world."

"You don't," said Phaon, "know my people. They have no desire at all to leave this world. At least, not in ships."

"Not in ships?" echoed Feltrie. "But how else could they leave it?"

"There is another way," put in Cyra. "There is the Roving."

"The Roving?"

Phaon's mouth twisted. "The glory of my people...and their curse. It is what makes them content to stay in buried Kothmar. For it is what makes them kings of the cosmos."

Bryant stared incredulously. "Your people call themselves cosmic kings, and yet don't leave their city?"

Phaon nodded somberly. "Yes. And it is true...they are lords of the universe, in their way. It is why they will not leave."

"But *you* left?"

Phaon said; "I had to. My daughter is a Forbidden Child."

Again Bryant said, "I don't understand. What is a Forbidden Child?"

"Food is scarce on this world.

Even with synthetics we barely produce enough to live on, and therefore a population cannot be allowed to grow. Each mating couple is told how many children they may have. We were allowed one. We had two. Cyra was the second."

"So?"

"So if she is caught and taken back, she will be sent to the House of Sleep. Destroyed." He made a sharp gesture with his hand. "Murdered."

"But," said Bryant, in absolute horror, "that's impossible. No civilized people…"

"Civilized people," said Phaon bitterly, "only think up a nicer name for what they do. Survival in Kothmar is not possible for too many people. Therefore the birth rate must be controlled. Otherwise, there would be too many, and all would have to leave Kothmar…and leave the Roving that is dearer than life."

He added, heavily, "My wife is dead, long before her time, but even that does not atone for Cyra. The child must be slain; otherwise more people would be tempted to break the law. We managed to lie about her for years, but at the last census we were found out."

"And you came here?"

"I was determined not to give up my daughter."

"But a thousand miles," said Bryant. "How did you survive the nights, without a dome?"

They all looked at him as though they did not understand him. And Cyra said,

"Father was with the Department of Engineers. He knew all the old ways. We didn't have…" Belath turned suddenly toward the door. "Listen. I thought I heard…"

They stood still and listened, and Bryant heard it too.

There were voices calling in the city, far and harsh and strident…the voices that a thousand star-worlds feared.

CHAPTER SIX

BRYANT'S HEART began to beat like a hammer against his ribs. The sweat broke out on him, first hot, then cold. He looked at Feltrie. A little color had come back into Feltrie's cheeks for a moment, but it was gone again now, leaving them ashen.

The voices called and answered in the distance, then, echoing, spreading out across the segment of the city nearest the blue court, where the shaft was to the surface.

Phaon lifted the weapon in his hands. His eyes had a look of despair, but they were steady. "They've followed us," he said.

"Not you," Bryant said. "Us. I've heard voices like that before. Those are Varkonides."

"But how?" asked Feltrie. "It was pitch dark; they couldn't have seen us."

"They're from Kothmar," said the boy. "Of course they are." He began to look around as though there was something important he had to find. Cyra stood still, frightened, but more composed.

Bryant said, "It must have been the light."

"What light?" said Feltrie. "The flash of light from the entrance, when it was open. You could see that a long way off. The metal cover is so dull and corroded it looks like part of the desert, and the dust covers it up again anyway, so it would take them a while to probe around and find it. But they'd know about where it was, if they saw the light."

The voices rang under the low vault. There was an exultant quality about them, like the baying of hounds, at once harsh and beautiful. The Varkonides loved to hunt.

Feltrie said, "They'll drive us until we're penned in against the dome, and then they'll narrow the perimeter, like that." He brought his two hands together as though he grabbed something between the palms. "The hell with a place like this where you can't even run."

"Listen," Bryant said to Phaon, "you've got to find somewhere to hide. They don't know you're here, and maybe…"

"Your thought carries no conviction."

"They're thorough," Bryant said. "They've got an instinct for it. And they'll loot, everything they can pick up or tear down and carry away."

He felt like a murderer. He looked at the girl Cyra, and he thought, I've killed the city and probably I've killed her too, and she's so little and pretty and already in trouble enough. Then he saw her give him a quick, warm glance, and realized that he had been broadcasting his private thoughts. He flushed, and then Phaon said,

"We'll have to go back into the tunnels. Quickly, before they reach this part of the city."

Bryant said, amazed, "You mean there's another way out?"

"All the cities are connected by a system of tunnels. Most of them are still operative. That's how we came from Kothmar."

Bryant said, "Let's go!"

THEY WENT, in a close little group, keeping to the narrow ways behind the houses. As they ran, Bryant questioned Phaon about their destination, and was given a quick, mental picture of a round, squat building on the other side of the amethyst avenue that bisected the city from the south as the yellow one did from the north. Bryant remembered it. He had not been able to open the huge metal doors, and there were no windows in the building to let him see what was inside. He had decided it was some kind of a power plant and probably dangerous, and he had let it alone.

"In the old days it was a busy terminal," Phaon said. "But my children and I are the first to use it in centuries."

"And there are other empty cities, like this one?"

"All are empty, except Kothmar."

They ran, and the cries of the Varkonides came nearer. Cyra began to falter. Bryant put his arm around her and pulled her on. They skirted the plaza, knowing that they would be seen if they tried to cross that open space. They came south of it, to the edge of the amethyst avenue, and this they were forced to cross.

"Wait," said Bryant, in the shelter of the houses. "I'll take a look."

He peered cautiously around the corner. He could see straight into the plaza, and down its long axis parallel to the line of stelae, and into the yellow avenue beyond. And there was a swift-moving line of dark figures, coming his way.

It was already too late.

He did not stop to do any thinking, because, he knew if he did he would lose what little courage he had left. Feltrie was the important one. Feltrie and the girl. They must not be caught. He said as much, very briefly, and Feltrie protested, but he knew Bryant was right. Bryant unslung the shock rifle from his shoulder.

"As soon as you see us well engaged," he said, "run for it, and make it fast. I'll hold their attention as long as I can."

Before he could change his mind, he left them and began to run back toward the plaza, crouching low and keeping as much as possible behind the buildings. He tried not to think about how scared he was, but that didn't work, so he fixed his mind on how many Varkonides he was going to kill with his shock beam notched up to lethal voltage. He thought about Grach Chai and how much he hated him and what he was going to do to him if he got the chance.

It still didn't work. He was scared. He was so scared he did not think he could keep going, but he did. He reached the back of one of the white buildings that fronted on the plaza, and he climbed through a window into the lofty marble silence and ran in a sudden drumroll of echoes made by his own feet. He reached a tall window in the front and looked out.

The Varkonides were entering the plaza, lean olive-green warriors decked out in the fancy harness they loved so much that they would not lay it aside even in battle, gorgets and breast-pieces and wide girdles plated with precious metal and flashing with precious stones, and every last one of them stolen. Grach Chai led the party, wearing the flashiest trappings of all. They were laughing. They were enjoying themselves. They were looking around and pointing and thinking of loot even while they hunted.

Bryant shouted out, "Grach Chai!"

He pressed the stud of his rifle and fired.

He did not hit Grach Chai, who was already close to the first of the line of stelae, and who instantly took shelter behind it. The loose formation of Varkonides exploded outward from its own center, and within a second there was not a Varkonid in sight except the one who had received Bryant's shot.

Bryant dropped to the floor. The spitting hiss of the Varkonid rifles sounded from outside, and the window aperture flickered with dancing blue flame.

Snake-like, Bryant slid on his belly along the marble floor to another window. He sprayed what he could see of the plaza with a hard burst and then dropped again.

Once more there was the sputter of blue flame. From the sound and color Bryant could tell about how far the rifles were notched up, and it was not far enough. Not far enough to kill, just enough to stun. They liked to take their enemies alive. It was more fun that way.

Sweat ran down Bryant's forehead and trickled cold and clammy into his eyes. There was a bad taste in his mouth. Goddamn you, Phaon, he thought, you'd better get them there safe, or...

Phaon's thought came clearly into his mind. *We are making the crossing now.*

Bryant closed his hand on the communicator in his pocket. *Okay*, he thought. *I'll pin them down. Luck.*

The Varkonides would be expecting him to return to the first window. Instead, he rose up and blasted them again out the same one. He made this a good one, spotting his targets. Then he flung himself down, but it was a losing game, and this time he didn't make it. A stunning shock caught him on the way. From light-years off he heard Phaon's thought, *We made it, we are safe across.* He thought there was a second voice, that said, *Live, Hugh, live! We'll find a way…*He thought it was Cyra's but he was not sure.

He was not sure of anything except that the darkness was all around him like the sides of a well, and there was no bottom.

CHAPTER SEVEN

HE WAS STILL in the marble room, but he was no longer alone. With the first light that came back to him Bryant could see a horde of dark, jewel-flashing forms, moving as in a mist. The light got brighter and the mist cleared, and everything jarred into focus, the sights, the sounds, the colors.

He was hanging by his wrists midway up the marble wall. His feet swung in free air, high above the floor, and above him ropes had been made fast to two widely separated carved projections, so that his body sagged like a tapestry from his outstretched arms. The vaulted room swarmed with Varkonides, busy, talkative, animated. He could see out into the plaza through one of the tall windows where he had done his firing, and there the loot was already piling high around the stelae.

Goodbye to Annamar.

And to me too, he thought. It hasn't even started yet, and already I'm sick. Did the others make it, all the way?

A sudden clamor of thoughtvoices in his mind. *Are you all right, Hugh, what is happening to you, we are safe in...*

No! he almost shouted. *Don't tell me. I may betray you. Stay safe. Get clear out of the city if you can.*

Phaon saying, *It is not my way to desert a friend.*

Desert, hell, what do you think I did this for? Feltrie and your daughter are the ones...

One of the Varkonides noticed that Bryant was conscious, and yelled to Grach Chai.

The Varkonid chief was on the far side of the room, talking to three of his lieutenants. He turned at once and crossed the marble floor and stood looking up at Bryant. He was handsome. He was splendidly built, powerfully muscled. His smooth olive-green skin set off the gorgeous trappings he wore. His eyes were large, slightly slanted, and as bright gold as the plaques that hung from his ears.

"Bryant," he said, and smiled. His teeth were pointed and very white. "Are you awake and ready to talk to me?"

"I have nothing to say," Bryant told him, slipping and slurring over the unaccustomed glottals of the Varkonid speech.

"Oh," said Grach Chai, "but you have. Bring a chair, there. Let him down. Fetch some food and drink."

It was done, so swiftly and smoothly that Bryant knew it had all been arranged beforehand, for some purpose of their own. Just the same, he was glad to sit and get away from the tearing strain on his arms and the feeling of helplessness. The ropes were not removed from his wrists, nor were they let go of for a minute.

"Go on, eat," said Grach Chai. "A man is nothing with an empty belly." He poured liquor into frail crystal glasses brought out of some looted house. "Here, drink up. Burn the cobwebs out of your brain."

He handed glasses around to his lieutenants, and they all drank, and Bryant drank too, without hesitation. The Varkonides were not poisoners. The liquor felt very good going down. He thought he would have a little more of it, not too much, but no food. Food did not seem at all a good idea.

"Why not?" asked Grach Chai, when he refused, and Bryant nodded at the high wall, and the ropes on his wrists.

"I haven't got too strong a stomach."

Grach Chai laughed. He could look very pleasant when he laughed. He turned to his lieutenants and said, "Bryant complains of his weak insides," and they laughed, too. Grach Chai leaned forward.

"Listen, Bryant," he said, "a man who can do what you did must have guts of steel. Tell me, how did you feel when you were hiding in the Cloud, hunting for our base? Were you shivering with fright?"

Bryant thought back. That was the first time he had been clear outside the galaxy, and he remembered the wild heart-stopping thrill when they had left the last of the fringing suns behind and he had looked out into the vast, the immense, the unthinkable gulf that lay before him, with Andromeda burning like a mighty torch at the end of it and the farther galaxies scattered across creation like misty star-webs. Then he had looked astern and been stricken dumb with the wheeling blaze of his own universe, a billion billion suns all hiving together in a single swarm.

He had run the scout-ship far out into the black sea that lies between the island universes, and he had raised the Cloud from its outer side, running in among its secret star-shoals from a direction whence nothing had come since God Himself walked that way, making the cosmos as He went.

After that it had been a kind of game, to find the hidden world of the Varkonides without getting caught themselves. Not an easy game, either, in a region unexplored and uncharted, where you never knew what you would find beyond the next sun, or behind the veils of nebulosity. But he could not recall that he had been very much afraid.

HE SAID SO to Grach Chai, and the Varkonid nodded, eagerly. "There was too much else to think about, wasn't there? Too much to see, to experience, and too much excitement in the game."

Bryant was forced to admit that it had not been dull. He and Bud Wallace and Feltrie in their tiny minnow of a ship, lurking among the wild suns and tracking the great Varkonid sharks little by little to their home world, and then sneaking in where no sane men would have tried, to land Feltrie and wait for him and then take off again.

It was the take-off that had gone wrong. He and Bud Wallace had been forced to leave the ship to rescue Feltrie, and Bud had not made it back. But Bryant had got the scout off the ground and gone belting out like a lunatic through the swarm of moons that fringed the planet. Since then, he had been running. And now he was caught.

"But you did it, Bryant," said Grach Chai. "That's the thing. You're a spaceman, a fighter. You don't belong with these fat pink men who make money on the safe worlds. You belong with us."

Grach Chai hitched his chair closer to Bryant. His eyes were like two hot drops of gold and the gold plaques swung from his ears, and the jewels in his harness dazzled Bryant's gaze.

"Listen, Bryant, I'll give you a ship of your own. We're raiding south along the Rim, far south into new sectors. We'll all get rich, and we'll have excitement enough for all, new suns, new worlds, new races, new women; new kinds of plunder. I won't ask you to go against your own friends. And you won't be alone with us, either. There are quite a few of your own race in the Cloud. Think about it, Bryant."

He thought about it. He thought about gold and glory and foreign suns. He thought about swooping like an eagle down out of the Cloud and running in to raid along the Rim, and he thought about a lot of things he would have been ashamed to put into words because they would have sounded strange in the mouth of a civilized man. He thought that underneath he was not too different from Grach Chai. And before he could think too much he said,

"No. Time has gone by for that sort of thing. It's too late. You've already been pushed to Magellan. The next push will be…" He shrugged. "Out."

"Then we'll explore Andromeda together," said Grach Chai. "You're a brave man. Don't make me kill you."

Bryant looked at him. "I know what you want, Grach Chai. And you ought to know I won't give it to you."

The Varkonid poured more liquor for them both and sat back, shaking his head.

"You know I can't let Feltrie get away with those microfilms. We're not quite ready for Andromeda yet. Listen, Bryant. We'll get him. There isn't any way he can get off this planet. We found your ship. We wrecked it. If he shows on the surface, my patrols will pick him up. If he's underground…well, we can go as far as he can. And we will. This is an ideal base, Bryant. It has so many possibilities I haven't even begun to count them yet. So you can't help Feltrie. You might as well help yourself."

"No," said Bryant, and drank his drink, and sighed.

"And you might as well tell me," Grach Chai said, "who else is in the city."

Bryant barely controlled a violent start. "What do you mean, who else?"

"Bring that stuff here," said Grach Chai, turning around. "Yes, that." A Varkonid picked up a bundle some distance away and brought it to Grach Chai, who opened it and spread out what was in it for Bryant to see.

"These were found in one of the houses. Somebody...two or three people, apparently...had been living there, and not centuries ago, either. Not earlier than this morning."

Bryant stared at the little heap of belongings. He sent the thought to Phaon, *Now they know. They have the things you left behind...*

"Who were they, Bryant? Where did they go?"

Bryant said, "I don't know."

"Are there other cities like this one? Inhabited cities?"

"I don't know."

"There's one building my men haven't been able to break into yet." He described the round terminal building. "What is it, and why is it locked?"

"I don't know," said Bryant.

"Well," said Grach Chai, "we'll find out." He looked at Bryant with genuine regret. "One last chance?"

"No," said Bryant, and his regret, too, was genuine.

Grach Chai shrugged. "Strip him," he said.

In the few seconds left while he still had the communicator, Bryant sent the frantic thought to Phaon, *Get out of Annamar, you can't help me. The Varkonides will take over this whole planet...you should warn Kothmar...*

He heard a faint, faint cry of *Hugh!* and he knew it was Cyra. Then the strong hands had torn his tunic away and the communicator with it, and he was all alone, and Grach Chai said, "Pull him up."

BRYANT LOST TRACK of time. He lost track of practically everything, except the dark Varkonid faces swimming in a bloody mist below him, and Grach Chai's voice, and pain. Of this last there was plenty. More than enough. And yet the Varkonides doled it out sparingly, so that he should not have a surfeit of it at any one time and thereby lose the full savor. They kept him conscious long after he thought he ought to be dead, and Grach Chai's voice was clear and loud in his ears, asking, asking, always asking.

Why give your life for Feltrie? He's a mercenary, a hired man. He's no friend you're bound to.

Where is Feltrie?

Who are the others, and where are they?

Why be a fool, Bryant? You can still have that ship. You can still fly with us instead of against us. Come on, Bryant. The freedom of the Rim is yours.

Why don't you take it?

In spite of their skill and their tender care, Bryant began to slip away from them into unconsciousness.

"All right," said Grach Chai. "Let him down."

Bryant had no feeling left in his arms at all, but he felt the floor come up under his feet, and then he passed out entirely.

When he came to he was all alone. He could hear voices and movement from the plaza outside. The Varkonides were still looting the city, and probably Grach Chai had gone off with his lieutenants to make an assault on the terminal building. They would be back. They were not through with him yet. Not while he was alive.

He was bound now at both wrists and ankles. His clothes lay where they had been thrown, not far away from him. Among the litter the Varkonides had left behind he saw a small sharp knife, the blade of which was stained with his own blood.

An idea began to shape dimly in his mind.

Sensation had returned to his arms. It was not a good sensation. Every nerve, muscle, bone, and joint was a separate and powerful agony. But he could move them. He began to crawl a little at a time to where the knife was. After a great deal of effort he got it between his teeth, and after a great deal more he was able to haggle apart a strand of the cord that held his wrists. Then he freed his feet.

Still Grach Chai had not come back.

Bryant pulled on his pants and tunic. The communicator was still in his pocket. The Varkonides had thought it of no value, and passed it by. Desperately he called out, hoping for an answer and afraid there would be one.

Phaon's thought-voice said tensely in his mind, *I was about to come and see if you were dead.*

Where are you?

Below, in the service levels. The others wait in the tunnel. Can you walk?

I think so. At least I'm free. Wait…No, it's all right, just someone in the plaza. Which way?

At the back of the hall you will see an archway. If you can get through it, there is a stair…

I'll get through it.

He almost didn't. His legs were like two pieces of wet string and the air kept turning dark around him. He still had the little knife, but he did not know what good it would do him if one of the Varkonides came in.

None of them did, and the million miles that lay between him and the arch were crossed at last. Beyond it there was a narrow hall that seemed to run for some distance on either hand, and the stair opened off it.

Come down, said Phaon.

He came down, staggering as fast as he could, into a place of empty marble vaults.

Here the records of Annamar were kept, but they are under Kothmar now. The history of our world lies under Kothmar. There is another stair. Come down.

He did. And now a door confronted him. He was in a space no larger than a coffin, and the way was barred, and from behind him, suddenly, impinging upon the blurry turmoil of his mind and sending a shooting chill through every nerve, there came a sound. A small sound. A soft sound. The quick scuffing of a shod foot against stone.

Phaon! Phaon! he cried. *I am followed. It was all a trap to make me lead them to you. Get away before...*

THE DOOR OPENED and Phaon pulled him through it, and shut it again, and set the lock.

They'll cut through it. With torches. A minute, two...

Let them. I know these levels. They do not.

But, said Bryant despairingly, *they are hunters.*

He followed Phaon into an Annamar he had never seen before.

Here were vast avenues, not of houses, but of machines. They stretched away on all sides, mighty structures of metal, towers, cones, cubes, truncated pyramids like a fantastic city in themselves, and the bare rock under his feet quivered with the steady thrust and drone of power. Here and there shapes moved in the distance, and denizens of these streets...servo-mechanisms that kept the machines and each other in repair.

This way, said Phaon.

He turned into a street of linked dynamos, and then began to weave in and out around the bases of the huge structures, as one might dodge among houses for shelter. And even in his daze of pain and worry, Bryant found time for wonder.

Why? All this power, everything in order, the city left just as it was...

It costs us nothing, Phaon said.

The controlled-fusion reactor is practically everlasting, and all this is self-containing. It is a safeguard for us, in case the dome of Kothmar fails...as other domes have failed. We have a place ready to receive us, without delay.

He paused and looked back along the gleaming avenues. *I think they have lost us. Hurry now...*

They fled, twisting and turning among the great machines, toward the entrance into the tunnels from which freight and supplies had been brought in the old days.

Phaon said, *I have taken counsel with Feltrie, and with Cyra. We must go back to Kothmar...*

Bryant caught his arm and pointed down an open space to a parallel avenue. *They're still with us. Grach Chai and two others, keeping abreast. They have more weapons, and they can run faster. We'll never...wait. Wait. Phaon! We have one advantage over them.*

He projected a thought ahead. *Cyra? Cyra!*

The answer came. *Yes, Hugh.*

Give your communicator to Feltrie. Hurry!

There was a brief silence, or rather blankness. Bryant and Phaon dodged among giant ducts that carried air to Annamar. How far now? Bryant asked, and Phaon said, *Just there, on this side of the pumping plant.*

Feltrie's thought came blundering into his mind. *I'm here. What is it?*

Listen, Jim. We've got to plan out something, and plan it fast.

The door to the tunnel lay just ahead. On his right hand, the Varkonides moved, swift secret shadows, behind the ducts. Once they were through that door, their way would lie open to Kothmar and the loot of a whole planet.

And the death of a world, not just the death of a city, would be on Bryant's soul.

CHAPTER EIGHT

THOUGHTS, flying thick and fast through his mind. Plans. Alternatives.

Okay, Hugh. When you come through the door you keep right on going. Cyra's getting ready. Just a minute now, stall around somehow, give us time!

Bryant stumbled, a thing he found very easy to do, and Phaon caught him and bore him up, and they went on more slowly toward the door.

Belath was thinking something dark and sullen in the background, but he could not hear what it was. Perhaps Belath himself was not conscious of it.

He could not see the Varkonides now. But he knew that they were there.

The door was in front of them, its metal grooved and scarred with centuries of use. Phaon put out his hand.

Now. Now! Watch out. Here we come, ready or not.

Steady. Play it straight, this is no time to get light-headed.

Ready or not, you shall be caught.

Oh, hell.

The door swung open.

There was a long lighted ramp beyond it, and at the foot of the ramp there was a slip or dock where a bullet-shaped monorail car lay waiting. To the left, beyond the car, was the terminal proper, a vast round cavern ringed with the mouths of tunnels, rayed with docks. From far overhead, dim and muffled down the lift shaft, came the thumpings and bangings of the Varkonides trying to penetrate the massive metal doors of the building above. Apparently they were afraid to blast lest they bring down the dome on their own heads. To the right was the arched darkness that led a thousand miles under rock and dust to Kothmar.

Nothing else was in sight. Nothing living, nothing human.

Bryant and Phaon passed through the door. They went down the ramp toward the car, Bryant sagging in Phaon's arms and the smaller man lurching and heaving as he struggled with the weight. They did not look back. They did not seem to know that they were followed.

It was quiet in that rocky place. The distant noises from above did not disturb that quiet.

The hatch of the car was open. Suddenly Cyra appeared in it. She called out urgently in her own language, beckoning them to hurry, to get in, pointing forward meanwhile as though someone was at the controls of the car, impatiently waiting.

Grach Chai called from behind them. "Bryant!" he said. "Stop where you are."

Bryant stopped. Phaon stopped. They turned, and Cyra put her hands up over her mouth.

Grach Chai and his two lieutenants passed through the doorway from the service level, their shock-rifles ready in their hands, their faces alight with pleasure.

Feltrie stepped from behind the back-swung leaf of the door and fired, twice.

Grach Chai dropped like a stone. The man next to him dropped. But the third one turned, before Feltrie could fire again.

Belath shot him in the back, from the opposite side of the door.

Phaon and Bryant came running up the ramp.

"They're not dead?" Bryant said.

Feltrie shook his head. "I did what you told me. But I don't see…"

"Grach Chai is more use to us alive. Help me get him up."

"Mine is dead," said Belath. He was staring down at the Varkonid, as though now that he had finally killed somebody, the sensation was not at all what he had expected.

Phaon explained, "Our weapons are old-fashioned and purely lethal. We have had almost no occasion to use them for many centuries, so we have not bothered to improve them."

HE BENT OVER to help Bryant with the Varkonid chief. Then Feltrie snatched something from its clip on Grach Chai's belt.

"Radio device," he said. "And it was open. There'll be others along."

They got Grach Chai between them and started to take him down the ramp, his long legs dragging. Belath still stood, staring down at the Varkonid he had shot.

"Come," said Phaon impatiently. "There is no time..."

Belath lifted his weapon and covered them all with it. His face was quite stony.

"No," he said. "We're not going back to Kothmar."

Silence again, in the great round cavern, while the three men stopped and looked at the boy and then at each other, with the unconscious Varkonid a dead weight between Bryant and Feltrie.

Feltrie said, "I think he means it."

"I mean it," Belath said. "I don't care what happens to them in Kothmar. I care about my sister."

Phaon moved toward him. "Put that away," he said, "and come on."

"I won't harm you, Father," Belath said. "But these others have brought nothing but trouble to us, and they deserve to die. If you wish them to live, take Cyra and go to one of the other cars. Let the strangers go to Kothmar if they wish, but take us to some other city." His spoken voice went up almost to the breaking point. "I will not go back and let them kill her!"

Phaon said desperately, "I thought you understood. Things have changed. There is no longer any place on this world where we could hide. These invaders will find us wherever we go. Our only hope is to rouse Kothmar to fight."

"Fight?" said Belath bitterly. "Our people, against these?" He pointed to the Varkonides. "It only means throwing ourselves into the same trap."

Cyra left the car and came running up the ramp. She had given her communicator to Feltrie, so Bryant could not understand her, but she spoke sharply to the boy, and Phaon said to Bryant,

"Go on to the car."

"No!" cried Belath, and fired into the air over Bryant's head.

"Oh, lord," said Feltrie. "What a time for him to pick to get difficult! Listen, Belath, did you ever hear of the Galactic Council? It resettles populations. Anyone who wants to leave Kothmar can do it. Including you, including your sister. There isn't any reason for them to kill her now!"

"I don't believe you," Belath said. He looked very young, very desperate.

"It's true," Bryant said. "If we live through this, we'll get you all away from here."

Phaon spoke to Cyra, and she turned to Bryant and smiled, a warm and fleeting thing. Then she walked up to Belath and took the tube-like barrel of his weapon in her two hands.

"All right," said Phaon. "Quickly, now."

Bryant and Feltrie dragged Grach Chai down the ramp and into the bullet-shaped car. In a second or two Cyra and Belath followed, and now she carried the weapon.

Phaon pressed a stud and the hatch closed. On a simple control panel a setting had already been made. Phaon closed a switch and the car began to move. It picked up speed so smoothly that Bryant was scarcely conscious of acceleration, and almost at once the car had plunged into the blackness of the tunnel, so that there was nothing beyond the ports to judge by; but from the way a particular pointer climbed on the board he was sure that they were going fast enough. He tried to forget all about the black tunnel and the bulk of a planet over his head and all the things that could happen if some tiny detail went wrong.

There were big padded seats. He and Feltrie bound Grach Chai with great care and made him fast in one of the seats. The Varkonid was still unconscious and would remain so for a while. Bryant took over his shock-pistol and a gold-handled knife. After that there was nothing to do but sit.

THEY SHARED out their rations, eating frugally because food was scarce in Kothmar and there was still the need to conserve. Feltrie returned Cyra's communicator. They talked for a while, about the Varkonides and what they would do, and the value of Grach Chai as a hostage. They talked about what this would mean to Kothmar, and about other worlds, and what it would be like to live under a sun and moon, in the free air.

"Not all of us are so far gone in the Roving that we are ready to forget all reality," Phaon said. "Some of us would have made contact with the men of the spaceport years ago, taking the chance that they would be friendly. But it was forbidden, lest Kothmar be destroyed, or the Roving stolen from us."

He shook his head. "Men fling themselves upon madness," he said, "and they will not give it up."

Bryant asked, "What is this that you call the Roving?"

"It is our life," said Phaon, "and our destruction. Because of it we never developed space-flight, and so were trapped here, a dying people on a dying world. Because of it we were able to survive even after we were forced underground, shut off forever from the sky. We do not need the sky. We do not need anything, except a little food. We live extravagantly, we are prodigals with life. Even these far-roving Varkonides are nothing beside us. And yet we die, never having really lived."

Bryant still had no idea of what the Roving was.

"You must experience it yourself," said Cyra. "No one can explain it to you."

"Do you enjoy it," he asked her, and she glanced sidelong at her father.

"Yes. Belath and I both...we are young, and there is no other outlet for us. If it were not for my father, we would be addicts like the rest. But he has taught us differently."

The car rushed on, through the dark tunnel under the crust of the world. They were all tired, emotionally worn, mentally oppressed. Bryant still suffered from what Grach Chai had done to him. He looked at the Varkonid, and wondered why in spite of that he did not hate him nearly as much as he had before.

Feltrie said, "There's one big question that nobody has answered yet."

"What's that?"

"I think you said that the Varkonides had destroyed our ship?"

"That's what Grach Chai told me."

"Uh huh. So that leaves two Varkonid cruisers, supposing they don't call for more to come. Now, in the first place, I don't think we can probably capture a cruiser, and in the second place, two men couldn't possibly fly it if we did."

"No," said Bryant.

"All right," said Feltrie. "So you tell me. Suppose Kothmar does fight, and suppose we even win...this skirmish, anyway. How do you and I get off this graveyard planet?"

Bryant did not give Feltrie any answer to that question. He did not have one.

CHAPTER NINE

THE SWIFT RUSH of the car through darkness began almost imperceptibly to slow.

Bryant felt the nerves prick and tighten in his stomach. Cyra's face was pale and unhappy, and Belath held tightly to her hand. Phaon kept glancing at them uneasily. Now that he was almost there, he seemed to be doubting the wisdom of this return to Kothmar.

Nobody said anything. Grach Chai, fully recovered now, sat and watched them with his bright yellow eyes, alert and wary.

"Luck of the game," he had said to Bryant. "I'd rather be up than down, who wouldn't? But you have to take it as it comes."

Bryant and Feltrie arranged his bonds so that he could walk, but would be hampered from any sudden action. He seemed amused by this.

"Do you think I'm dangerous enough to take on a whole city single-handed?" he asked.

Bryant said, "I wouldn't be a bit surprised to see you try."

Grach Chai looked at him. "I wasn't wrong about you, Bryant. You bore up proudly when we had you. My offer is still good. And because I'm on the wrong side of the balance now, I'll broaden it to include Feltrie. Why not? The microfilm is more important than the man."

He nodded toward the others. "They're a poor lot. Let them go their ways. Free me, and the three of us can go back together."

Bryant shook his head. Feltrie shook his head. Grach Chai sighed, and settled back to his patient waiting.

The car moved slower and slower. It came out of darkness into light and the close walls of the tunnel sprang apart into a huge round terminal much like that of Annamar, except that it was larger. The car slid gently into its dock and was still.

Phaon reached up and closed the control board. He turned and smiled at Cyra and Belath, but it was only the shell of a smile, and there was nothing under it but fear. He opened the hatch and stepped out onto the dock.

Cyra and Belath followed him, and then Feltrie came, and Bryant, with the tall Varkonid walking between them.

There was no one on the dock. The terminal was as silent as the one they had left, the cars lying idle in the slips, the mouths of the waiting tunnels dark and still. Some of them were barred, as though the way beyond was blocked or dangerous. Nothing moved, except themselves.

They walked along the dock to the central island. There was the shaft of a lift there, and they entered it, and were taken up slowly past the lower levels and into a building. There was no one in the building. They passed out of it and into the street.

For a moment Bryant felt that they had moved in a circle and were back in Annamar. But then he saw that this city was much larger, and the plants that helped to keep the oxygen balance were trimmed and tended, and the houses had a look of being lived in.

Only there was no one in the streets. And it was quiet, as quiet as empty Annamar.

"Is it night?" asked Bryant.

Phaon said, "No. If it were night, the shutters of the sleeping-rooms would be closed, and there would be some people in the streets."

Cyra said, "It is the time of the Roving. By law, certain hours are for the work that must be done, and certain others are for food and sleep, and during those hours the central control is locked. Otherwise we would spend all our time in our other lives, and soon we would die. The mind and body can only stand so much."

"My home is not far," said Phaon. "Come and learn how we use our cleverness for our own destruction."

"But," said Bryant, amazed, "the warning. The Varkonides. Shouldn't we…"

"There is no one here to warn," said Phaon. "You do not understand. This is the time of the Roving, and we six are the only souls in Kothmar."

They walked through the streets, across bright pavements and under the walls of colored houses. Nothing moved, and several times through the open jalousies Bryant saw men and women and even children lying as though they were dead on padded couches, and each one wore a crystal circlet on his head, a circlet glowing with an eerie light.

IN THE CENTER of the city, reaching almost to the highest part of the dome, there was a slender tower unlike anything in Annamar. At its top was a device shaped like a huge ring, and made of crystal, and it, too, glowed with the same pale luminescence.

"That is the central control," said Phaon. "The transducer impulse is broadcast from it to all parts of the city, to be picked up and amplified by the individual receivers." He touched the small communicator that hung at his neck. "These were the start of it. When our scientists solved the problems of mental projection, it was only a step farther in principle to the Roving. Instead of projecting only simple thought, the transducer makes it possible to project the whole mind, the consciousness, wherever it may wish to go."

He turned aside and came to the doorway of a house the color of aquamarine. "Please," he said, "to enter."

They did so, and still they had not met a single person. "Isn't anyone waiting for you?" asked Bryant. "Police, I mean, watching in case you came back." He looked at Cyra. "I thought..."

"What need?" said Phaon. "We are here. It will be known. In the meantime, there is no hurry. Nothing is done in haste in Kothmar."

He motioned them to couches in the main room. Bryant and Feltrie between them had kept Grach Chai informed of what was going on, and now he disposed himself with considerable eager interest for the Roving.

"Do you mean," he asked, through Bryant, "that I—or rather the thinking part of me—will be able to leave my body and go wherever I will it?"

"With the freedom and the speed of thought." Phaon held up one of the crystal circlets. "This amplifier picks up the transducer impulse and transmits it directly to the brain, where the electro-cohesive matrix of the thinking personality undergoes a vibratory shift that frees it completely from the bonds of the flesh, for as long as the transducer continues to be active."

"Who knows?" Grach Chai said. "Perhaps we shall take this for ourselves."

"Perhaps," said Phaon grimly, "that would be the solution to the whole problem of the Varkonides."

He placed the crystal circlet on Grach Chai's brow and settled him on the couch, and pressed a stud. Instantly the circlet glowed. Grach Chai's face took on a momentary expression of stunned surprise, and then it became perfectly blank, remote and secret as the face of a corpse.

"Are you ready?" Phaon asked.

Bryant glanced uneasily at Feltrie, and then they both said. "I guess so." They lay back on the couches. Cyra brought a circlet and put it on Bryant's head. It felt cold against his flesh. She smiled and said, "It is quite safe." She pressed the stud.

Bryant felt himself caught and flung away in a rush of cosmic wind. Cyra vanished. Everything vanished. He raced headlong through oblivion, and then there was light again, and he hung poised and weightless, bodiless and free, above the surface of a world.

The world was old and rusty. On a wrinkled red plain he saw a spaceport with two black cruisers on it, and in a fold of the humpy hills there was the wreckage of a little ship. The world was Midway. The ancient sun brooded in the sky, remembering the days of its hot youth. There was no sign of Annamar or Kothmar or any other place of life. The matrix of energy that was, or had been, Bryant found little interest in it.

He turned outward and began to rove.

He could see the scattered stars now as he had never seen them. He could perceive them as suns, from the outside, just as he had before, but he could also perceive the forces that made them live. He could perceive the stripped and primal particles of matter, and he could follow them as they surged through the roar and thunder of the solar furnace, beaten and hammered into new substances and torn apart again with raving bursts of energy. It was unthinkably terrifying and magnificent. Fascinated, he hovered near a great blue star and watched for—how long? There was no time. Seconds, centuries. Then he wearied of it and drifted on.

The rim of the galaxy wheeled beneath him and was gone. Ahead there was a vast dark; and at the end of it—as he had seen it before in some other half-remembered existence—was another galaxy, burning bright.

Andromeda.

He wanted to go there.

He went.

Again there were suns and moons and planets and great looping nebulae and the sinister blacknesses of dust-clouds. He flittered moth-like from star to star, and then an ice-blue planet caught his fancy. He dropped toward it, and it was all watery, with only islands of low green land. The seas were very beautiful, silvery and warm under a milky sun. He went low to the water, and something moved in it, and he entered into that something and became one with it, a sharer in every thought and emotion, but possessing no power to influence.

He swam in the warm sea. His body was sleek and very powerful, covered with a close pale fur. He was hunting. He was not hungry. He was not seeking food. He was hunting for an enemy.

HE SWAM TOWARD the green archipelago. When he was on the surface he breathed air through his nostrils. When he sank below, slipping through a forest of tall bright weed, he closed his nostrils and used gills. His swift motion through the water was a sensuous pleasure, almost like flying. He could walk erect on the land, but he did not like that.

He moved stealthily in the shallows until he saw someone stir in the fringes of the silver-green, silver-pink forest that grew beyond the beach. Then he became excited, and his muscles quivered with the pleasure of what was coming. He approached the beach, quite silently, and left the water. His hand closed on a heavy stone.

The enemy was in the forest. The enemy had left behind the warm places of the sea. The enemy built his house on the naked land. The enemy had forgotten how to use his gills. The enemy hardly ever swam. The enemy was evil.

The enemy was small. It was only a cub, carrying a little basket of plaited rushes. It looked up at him as he rushed, and made a thin screaming, and was still. It was small, but it was the enemy, and to kill the enemy was good.

He looked down at it, and then he dropped the stone and glanced from side to side, and slunk back to the water.

Behind him the parents of the cub came crying to the edge of the water, but they stopped there. He sank out of sight and swam away. He had killed an enemy. It was good to kill what was wrong and unnatural, what left the mother ocean to stand tall on the land. It was good.

He swam deep, deep in the ice blue fathoms. There was a valley there, filled with silver bubbles, bright with slender weeds. There was a house there that he had built out of coral stone. He had an evil thought as he swam toward it. He thought the sun was let in upon it, and the weed was shriveled black, and the tall parents of the cub were tearing down the stones.

He swam in terror toward the valley.

Bryant left him. He—his mind—was swept on into the vast star jungle, past smoking suns, brooding blackness of clouds, a cluster...

He was on a world of that cluster, on a high hill, and it was sunset. He and his fellows—furred, grotesque, mighty— waited. The sun dropped. The sky darkened. The million stars of the cluster sky exploded like fireworks into being, and Bryant and his fellows raised their arms and howled.

He swept away from that, on toward another world, and another, so quickly that the worlds, the scenes, the bodies he briefly lived in, were like fast-flicking frames of a high-speed film.

Worlds of crystal in which he too was crystalline and sessile but thinking; worlds where he was a barbarian riding a strange, high beast in headlong charge down shadowy gorges; phantasmagoria of planets of nightmare and of beauty, serene loveliness and horror undreamed; terror and greed and lust and joy...

Suddenly, the same cosmic wind that had caught him up before caught him now. Andromeda dwindled and became a distant flame, and then was lost entirely in the sullen glare of a red sun. A wrinkled desert rushed up to meet him, fast, fast...

HE STARTED UP with a cry. Cyra stood beside him. He was back in Phaon's house. Feltrie and Grach Chai were rising on their couches, too, the circlets dull and dead around their brows.

They looked at each other with dazed eyes.

"I was an emperor," Feltrie said. "Under a double star, in the heart of a golden nebula. We weren't human. It was terrible, and wonderful. I had only just started..."

Phaon said, "The time is over."

Bryant said, "Good God, no wonder your people think themselves kings of the cosmos!"

"Where did you go?" asked Feltrie.

"I went to Andromeda."

"What did you find there?" said Grach Chai softly.

"Death. Beauty. Fear."

"What else is there?" The Varkonid shivered all over, and his eyes were very far away. "Now I see why these people care for nothing else. To have the whole cosmos open to you—universe after universe—a man could not come to the end of it if he lived ten thousand years—and with no danger, no effort, and always something new. My God, Bryant, if my people were to get hold of this…"

He sprang up. He sprang toward Phaon, who was closest to him. But he had forgotten that he was hobbled, and he fell. For a moment his face was a mask of pure ferocity. Then his attention, and everyone else's, was brought sharply to the door, where a file of men were entering.

There were eight of them, and one in the lead. The eight had weapons of the sort Belath had used on the Varkonid back in Annamar. The ninth was apparently an official.

He spoke to Phaon, looking with surprise and alarm at the strangers. He spoke very sharply, and Phaon showed his teeth in a bitter smile.

"He reproaches me," he said to Bryant, "for compounding my other sins by bringing strangers into Kothmar, a thing which is utterly forbidden. What he, and the Council of Kothmar, do not yet realize is that the end of one time has come, and the beginning of another. They are no longer in control."

It took exactly one hour and sixteen minutes by Bryant's wrist chronometer to prove that Phaon was wrong.

CHAPTER TEN

THE COUNCIL of Kothmar was small. It was composed of old men and old women, who knew a few simple basic truths and would not be turned from them. Things were as they were. Things would remain as they were. The ways of Kothmar were the right ways, and there were not going to be any others. The Council would not permit them.

They reminded Bryant strongly of the Andromedan who had chosen to cling to his gills, and who would not permit anyone else to do otherwise if he could help it.

The Council was not surprised that Phaon had returned. They had been expecting him. There was no food in the abandoned cities, and no survival on the surface, so eventually anyone insane enough to run away from Kothmar was forced to return. There was no escape from justice.

Cyra was to go, as the law required, to the House of Sleep. But now she would not go alone. The strangers would accompany her. Strangers were forbidden in Kothmar, for the safety of the city, and there was no food for them and no place in the economy.

"But what about the Varkonides?" cried Bryant, pointing to Grach Chai. "His people. We brought him to you a captive, so that you would have a bargaining point—aren't you going to use him?"

"We do not need him," said the Speaker of the Council.

"Do you think you can just ignore these people? Pretend they don't exist?" Bryant was furious. He looked around the semi-circle of councilors, cosmic kings in their other lives, possessing the universes, but in this life possessing nothing but stubborn complacency. "The Varkonides," he said, "will tear down the city over your heads while you lie dreaming on your couches."

"How will they reach us?" said the Speaker. "It is a simple matter to destroy the tunnel."

"You'll be cut off from Annamar."

"There are other cities."

"They'll search the planet till they find you. They'll be after loot and vengeance both, if you kill Grach Chai."

"Let them search," said the Speaker. "They will weary of it in time."

And Bryant could see that that might very well be true. Desperately, he said,

"Then you won't even help us to complete our mission? I've explained to you what it means to the Frontier..."

"This is not our affair. We do not feel obliged to become involved in it."

"All right," said Bryant disgustedly. "But at least let us go. Give us surface armor and weapons, and we'll take our chances." He put his arm around Cyra. "We'll take her with us. There's no need to kill her. There are plenty of worlds beyond this one, even without the Roving."

The Speaker of the Council said with obstinate patience, "Our law must be upheld for the safety of the community. It is obviously impossible to let you go upon the surface. If even one of you survived, the location of Kothmar would be known to everyone. No. There is nothing to fear in the House of Sleep, no pain, no ugliness. It is over quickly."

He turned to Phaon. "And you, who are chiefly to blame for all this, will go too. You have always been a troublemaker, Phaon. We cannot be patient any longer."

Phaon said savagely, "Is this your idea of justice? What about the people of Kothmar? Shouldn't they have something to say about how their lives are ordered? Perhaps some of them would prefer to leave, and live like men in the open. Have you any right to stop them?"

"Yes," said the Speaker, "as we did before, and as we will do whenever it is necessary, for the safety and preservation of Kothmar. And I greatly fear, Phaon, that your son will follow you in time to the House of Sleep, because of your upbringing. But for the present we will let him live. And now..."

"You, sir," said Bryant, "are a sanctimonious murderer. And the day will come..."

For the first time a flash of genuine anger showed in the old man's face.

"You were not asked to come here," he said. "You forced your way in, unwanted. Suppose I forced my way onto your world and told you that your traditions of centuries, your whole way of life, must all be overthrown in a minute, and my way adopted instead? How would you treat me?" He spoke to the guard. "Let the sentence be carried out."

HE TURNED AWAY and began to discuss with the Council the most effective means of blocking the tunnel to Annamar. Belath had moved back into an alcove, almost out of sight, his face very white and stony. The guard formed around the five who were condemned and marched them out of the marble council hall into the plaza.

This was much larger than the plaza at Annamar, and the tower of the Roving rose in the center of it. Feltrie looked at it and said,

"I guess you can't blame them. I mean, if I had that, I wouldn't risk losing it if the whole galaxy fell in pieces around me."

Bryant thought that that was true. Even one life is so precious that a man will go to any lengths to keep it, and the folk of Kothmar stood to lose not one but many lives, if anything happened to upset their ways.

They passed the tower in somber silence, walking close together within the circle of the guard. They all seemed stunned by what had happened, and Bryant was unable to grasp the fact that he was actually on his way to execution. He looked in a sort of dumb horror at his feet, marching steadily toward death, and then at Cyra. And she looked at him with eyes that shone with tears, and whispered, "I am sorry..."

In a doleful tone suitable to a condemned man, Grach Chai said, "The boy is following us behind the buildings. I think he has a weapon. If you could arrange it to free my hands…"

His ankle bonds had already been removed by the guard, when they took him from Phaon's house. Bryant saw Feltrie's eyes brighten, and his own spirits rose. It didn't look like much of a chance, but it was better than perishing meekly like so many sheep in this alien city.

The guards did not wear communicators, but Phaon and Cyra still had theirs, so they could talk to Bryant. He gave them some rapid mental instructions, and then said in a sad tone to Grach Chai,

"When we pass the corner of this building, the girl will faint. Catch her."

They walked on the white paving of the plaza, and the people of Kothmar passing by looked at them from a distance, curious but aloof. The tower rose up toward the dome, the great crystal tube that crowned it dull and lightless now. The kings of the cosmos were only men and women now, busy with the day's work. He wondered where they had all been, and what wonders they had seen, and what splendid journeys they were looking forward to when the crystal glowed again.

They passed the corner of the building, and Cyra faltered and fell against Grach Chai.

He caught her as well as he could with his bound hands, and Bryant turned instantly and reached out for the girl. There was a brief confusion, during which Grach Chai's hands were hidden by Cyra's body, and Cyra's hands by Bryant. When the guard, which had been forced to halt, got them separated again, the Varkonid's hands were free.

He brought them smashing into the astonished face of a guard, and then things happened fast. Cyra dropped to the ground out of harm's way. Bryant landed a terrific uppercut on the jaw of the nearest guard. He grabbed for the man's weapon as he went down, missed it, and saw Feltrie grapple with a guard and go rolling with him on the ground, beating the man's head against the marble paving. Close by Bryant's shoulder Grach Chai whooped out a war-cry and sent the little men of Kothmar staggering under his blows.

Bryant knocked another one down himself and then bent again for the weapon. For this first moment of surprise, guard and prisoner were too closely entangled for weapons to be used by those not engaged, but this would not go on for long. Bryant hoped that Belath would see his cue and take it.

He did. Even as Bryant got his hands on the unfamiliar weapon he heard Belath shout, and then a missile went singing over his head and into the breast of a guard who had backed off and sighted on Phaon. The man fell, and his shot went wild, catching one of his fellows. Phaon snatched his weapon and crouched on one knee, pumping shots with such terrible grimness and inaccuracy that Bryant made him stop and take Cyra to where Belath was running toward them down the open way between buildings. There were now four guards left on their feet. Bryant fired at them and one fell. The other three dropped their weapons and ran.

Feltrie and Grach Chai armed themselves, and they turned to join Phaon. Bryant realized that the advantage they had had was only partly due to their superior size and strength. It was chiefly because the men of Kothmar had never actually fought before and were horrified by the violence of it.

THE PEOPLE on the plaza were now in wild turmoil, crying out and running for shelter, or staring in shocked disbelief at the bodies of the guards and the red stains appearing on the white unsullied paving. And now Belath whirled suddenly and began firing back the way he had come, and Bryant saw a small detachment of guards running in the next street over. They took shelter immediately, and began to fire.

"They came after me," said Belath. "I knocked one down and took his weapon right after they took you away. I knew I'd have only a few minutes—what now?"

"Into the building," said Bryant.

They ran, ducking low. Missiles spattered against the marble wall, closer than Bryant liked. The plaza was filling with people, and many of them were armed men, apparently summoned in haste by the fleeing guards. Warriors or not, a city full of them were quite able to subdue four men and a boy.

An idea, which had been simmering in Bryant's mind, came to a full boil. "Up to the roof. I think there's a way to beat them..."

There were few people in the building, and what there were did not try to stop them. Phaon led them up broad marble stairs to the upper levels, and finally up a narrow stair of stone to the roof. Now there was nothing above them but the dome, and the slim tower of the Roving stood up against it with its crystal tube.

"Who's the best shot? Grach Chai? Feltrie? With a missile weapon. Feltrie? Okay. See how close you can come to that crystal ring without actually hitting it. Grach Chai, you and Belath hold the door there." He glanced over the parapet. The plaza was jammed, and the bodies of the fallen were being carried away. Somebody shouted, and missiles went snarling through the air, but the angle was bad and none of them even came close. "All right," said Bryant. "Now."

Feltrie drew a bead on the tower and pressed the firing stud. The missile whacked with a ringing sound against the tower, just under the crystal. It flattened and fell.

"Another," said Bryant. "Give 'em a couple, so they understand. But for God's sake don't hit it."

Feltrie gave them a couple. Phaon's face was white and he moved his lips nervously, looking up at the tower. From the plaza below came a shriek, and then a groan of agony. Grach Chai fired very fast, three or four times, down the stairs. Then there was silence.

"Tell them," said Bryant to Phaon, "that if they want to continue their Roving, they must listen to us. Keep down, behind the parapet."

Phaon kept down. He shouted to the men below in the plaza. After a while there was an answer.

"They will listen. They ask what we want."

"Tell them we only wish to leave Kothmar. Tell them we will smash the crystal instantly if a shot is fired, or they try to rush us. But if they will hear us out, and help us, nothing will happen to it."

Phaon told them that. Again there was an answer. "The Speaker of the Council is down below," Phaon said, and Bryant's mind worked feverishly, looking ahead.

"Tell him to come up," he said. "Alone. Tell him he won't be harmed."

As they waited, Feltrie looked at Bryant puzzledly and said, "Leave Kothmar? Where can we go?"

"Back up onto the surface here," said Bryant.

"To freeze to death? There's nothing up there but the two Varkonid ships!"

Grach Chai smiled. "My men will welcome us, I'm sure."

"I'm sure they would," said Bryant, "but we're not going to your ships. And you're still our prisoner. I'll take your weapon now."

Grach Chai looked at him levelly. Bryant added, "Feltrie is behind you. You can't get us both."

Grach Chai shrugged, grinned mirthlessly, and handed over the weapon.

Feltrie said, "Where are we going, on the surface?"

"You'll find out later and it's our only chance, and shut up for now," said Bryant.

The Speaker came then, reluctantly, angry and bewildered and more than a little frightened by the sudden upheaval in the orderly existence of Kothmar.

"Now then," said Bryant to Phaon, "tell him we're going up to the surface. Explain that we want armor, food, and water. Are there vehicles for surface use? If so, we want one."

The Speaker said that there were, although they had not been used for very many years, and would need servicing.

"Get them at it," Bryant said to Phaon. "Explain that when everything is ready we will leave this roof and go to the entrance shaft, and from there to the surface. Explain carefully that the Speaker goes with us as surety, and that he will be released as soon as we are safely out of Kothmar."

Phaon explained. And then there was a time of waiting, a time of tension, in which gloomy and foreboding thoughts went through Bryant's head.

His idea was simple and desperate. They were lost, if they stayed here. But on the surface, in the old spaceport, the emergency radio for world-wrecked star-ships might still be working. If it was, they could call the nearest civilized star.

If it wasn't, or if the Varkonides caught them, there was no hope at all.

They waited, and the three men from the outer world looked up at the tower whose power made sleeping men into cosmic lords.

"It's like a drug," Feltrie said. "Destructive, but so wonderful you don't care. You know what? We ought to smash it."

"No," said Bryant. "We can't shoot everybody in the city. They'd tear us to shreds. And besides…"

"Besides what?" said Feltrie.

"Never mind." said Bryant.

Grach Chai looked at him, and smiled.

The waiting time came to an end, and they and their ancient vehicle stood free in the bitter air of the surface, under the dull red eye of the sun, and the shaft of Kothmar closed behind them.

They moved off, Phaon and his son and daughter, Bryant, Feltrie and Grach Chai, into the thousand miles of dust and nothing that lay between them and the spaceport above Annamar—and the Varkonides of Grach Chai.

CHAPTER ELEVEN

THEY LAY HUDDLED in the night and the cold stars looked down upon them.

"We were crazy," Feltrie said.

"Yeah," said Bryant.

Grach Chai appeared to shrug inside his armor. "It's better than the House of Sleep."

"For you, yes," said Feltrie. "Even if you should die, you can die laughing at us. But for Bryant and me…"

"You're alive, aren't you?"

Feltrie grunted. "If you can call this living."

Grach Chai smiled. "Anyway, you're not absolutely dead. So you're still better off." He settled himself against the side of the truck. "Guard me well, and envy my unbroken slumber."

The truck shuddered in the gusts of wind. Bryant felt very tired, but he could not rest. Even in the protective armor, the bitter cold gnawed at him. The night was a howling beast, a thing of dread and terror. He had never seen the night here before except from the warm and lighted shelter of the spaceport domes. The wind was incredible. It screamed and howled around the low body of the truck and tried to bury it in dust, and when that did not work it tried to blow it over. It sucked the heat away from the truck's interior, and it pounded on a man's courage with a great cold shattering fist, and above it there was only blackness and the uncaring stars.

This was the second night. There would be one more. He did not know whether they could stand it.

Someone moved, close to him. It was Cyra. "Shall we die after all?" she asked him.

He said, "I don't know."

She leaned her armored shoulder against his, in a gesture of comfort and affection. After a while he thought she slept.

"What about it?" said Feltrie. "Is there any chance at all?"

Bryant looked at Grach Chai. He seemed to be asleep. So did Phaon and Belath. He said,

"The radio was left in the old spaceport, I'm sure of that. Not only for use of possibly disabled ships, but because we thought we'd be coming back pretty soon. It should be able to raise another civilized star and bring cruisers here fast, if we can reach it."

"If. And of course the Varkonides are camping on the port."

"Yeah. But one man might sneak past them at night, and get out the call for help."

Feltrie thought it over. "You figure to be that man?"

Bryant shrugged. "We'll settle that tomorrow night when we get near there. But I know the spaceport better than you do, so..." He added after a moment. "When I do go, you hang onto Grach Chai tight. You might just be able to buy your lives with him, in a pinch."

They haggled briefly over who was to take first watch this night. Feltrie got it. He sat where he could watch Grach

Chai. Bryant scrunched around, stiff and chilly in his armor. He did not think he could possibly sleep. But he did, and the last thing he thought of before he fell under the dark wave was how much he had come to hate this world, and the beautiful city of his youth. It had turned into a stifling trap, bringing him death instead of safety.

He dreamed about it. He was back in Annamar, only he was very big and the dome was very small, set over him like a turtle shell. There were sudden noises in it, and motion. He struggled to see what they were, but there was a weight on him, and then a tremendous crash on the dome directly over his head that knocked him senseless.

When he could see again he was back in the dim interior of the truck, with everyone sleeping. Cyra had moved until she was lying across his chest, and that was the weight he had felt. Otherwise everything was all right, except that his head ached—

And except that Feltrie, who should have been sitting up awake, now lay quietly on the floor. And Grach Chai was gone.

BRYANT LIFTED Cyra from him. She murmured sleepily, but did not wake. He went to Feltrie, shining a light in his face. Feltrie groaned and blinked his eyes. It was quite a while before Bryant could get any sense out of him, and even then he could not say what had happened.

Grach Chai must have been shamming sleep all the while, waiting for a moment when Feltrie's attention was drawn elsewhere or was dulled by exhaustion. Then he had struck Feltrie down. Bryant remembered the noises in the dream, and the stunning crash. He must have tried to get up., but Cyra had weighed him down, and Grach Chai had hit him too, on his helmet.

Feltrie began to feel around wildly under his armor. "They're gone," he said. "The micro-films. He must have taken them."

Bryant shook his head in black despair. "That's fine. And he can lead his men now straight to Kothmar, barely pausing to fix us on the way." He swore, to keep from crying. They had been through so much for those damned microfilms, and now they would not even live to say they had shot them. "And he must have heard us talk about the spaceport radio, too."

Feltrie said, "I'm sorry. But I wasn't asleep. I was— watching *that*, out there—" jerking his hand toward the outer night, "—and thinking about home. I guess he moved so fast I just didn't hear him."

"Well," said Bryant, "maybe we can still catch him. The truck can go faster than he can walk."

But he had not really allowed himself to hope, and so he was not particularly amazed or downhearted when they discovered that Grach Chai had succeeded in sabotaging the truck.

Bryant looked into the deadly blackness of the night that still had hours to go before dawn. "I'll just have to go after him," he said. "On foot."

"But you will die out there alone," said Cyra, who was awake now. "Stay here, Hugh. He will not make it, either, no one could. Why must both of you die?"

"Because I don't trust Grach Chai to lie down and perish. And the only chance we have in the world to survive is to catch him before he can reach his own men."

He took rations and water, and ammunition for the weapon. He kissed Cyra's cold lips, and shook hands with Phaon and the boy. To Feltrie he said, "Get 'em working to repair the truck as soon as it's light. Make believe I'm going to catch him."

Feltrie said, "Luck." He added, "There's one thing that puzzles me."

"What's that?"

"Why didn't Grach Chai kill us when he had the chance?"

"I don't know," Bryant said, and walked away from the truck, in the black cold tearing wind.

And there was desolation under the dim stars.

He tried not to think.

The armor was heavy and cumbersome. It chafed and impeded him, but as against the lunar chill it was frail as tissue paper, even with the heat control turned up full. Blown dust whispered over the faceplate of his helmet. The truck was lost behind him. Grach Chai was lost somewhere ahead. Apart from them nothing lived on the whole vast surface of this dead and silent world.

He walked.

Dawn came, a slow trickle of red light oozing through the night like blood through a dark bandage. It spread with glacial slowness across the plain, giving a gradual illusion of warmth. The wind dropped. It was day.

And day went on forever.

He walked. He ate and drank, and rested, and walked on, following his compass toward Annamar.

Just before noon he thought he saw a dark moving speck on the restless red, far in front of him and to his right. He followed it all through the long afternoon, and he thought he was gaining on it. By the time the crimson sun touched the horizon he had almost begun to hope. Then by the last of the light he saw a ridge of low rocky hills, and knew that they were a spur of the mountain chain north of the spaceport. The distant figure moved in among them and disappeared.

Bryant sat down in the dust, in the middle of the plain. The wind rose and the darkness came.

After a while Bryant ate and drank some water, and got to his feet again. He began to walk toward the hills.

All that night he dragged himself among the chalky boulders and the rotten stone, up and down. He fell often, and several times he passed out for short periods, but he did not stop. By now he was beyond stopping. He was beyond the conscious thought and reason that would lead to a decision to stop. The rocks broke some of the force of the wind, and the footing was firmer than the desert. When the dull dawn came again in to the sky he had reached the edge of the scarp. Far, far in the distance across the plain he could see the pylon of the spaceport.

DIRECTLY BELOW HIM, Grach Chai sat at the foot of the scarp, eating and drinking in a sheltered place before he set out on the last part of his journey.

Bryant lifted his weapon. Grach Chai looked up and saw him, and raised his hands. His voice came thin on the cold air.

"I'm not armed. Come down."

Bryant hesitated, fingering the trigger-stud. He thought of Feltrie and himself, still alive when Grach Chai could easily have killed them.

He said, "You took a weapon from the truck. Where is it?"

"It was heavy. I threw it away. Come down, Bryant, and eat."

Bryant lowered his weapon. He moved down the face of the scarp, lurching and sliding in the dust.

Grach Chai watched him. "I didn't think you could catch me," he said, and smiled. "You should have been a Varkonid."

He had not risen. Bryant stood in front of him, the weapon held loosely at the ready.

"Give me back the films, Grach Chai."

"I threw them away, too. In the dust, the desert, I don't think anyone will ever find them. Be satisfied, Bryant. Feltrie still has what information is in his head, and his head is still on his shoulders. It evens things up. Fair enough?"

Bryant asked, "Why didn't you kill us?"

"We have fought together," Grach Chai said. "A comrade in arms is no fit subject for murder." He held out his water bottle. "Here."

Bryant sat down. He drank from Grach Chai's bottle and gave it back. He shared with Grach Chai some of the rations he had brought.

"You will not change your mind and come with me?" asked Grach Chai.

"No."

Grach Chai got up. "I'm sorry, Bryant. Well, I'm going."

Bryant lifted his weapon again until it centered on Grach Chai's chest. "No," he said. "Oh, no, you're not going to get your men and ships and bring them here, and on to Kothmar. I'll have to kill you."

Grach Chai stared at him, with an incredulous expression, and then he said,

"You think I want Kothmar now?"

Bryant nodded. "A fine base for Varkon. You said so yourself. Yes, you want it."

Grach Chai exclaimed with sudden violence, "Why, gods of space, man, for the loot of twenty Kothmars, for a hundred bases, I wouldn't let my men try the Roving! Or even hear about it!"

Bryant held his weapon steady, and said nothing.

"Listen," said Grach Chai. "You know the Varkonides. We're a star-roving folk and always will be, mad to learn what's beyond the next nebula. If I took the Roving to Varkon, none of us would ever fly a ship again! No, that thing could ruin Varkon. If we go to Andromeda, it'll be in our own bodies, our own ships!" He added, "And if you're wise, Bryant, you'll forget the Roving too."

Bryant looked at him with the steady stare of exhaustion. He said, "You mean that you'll just take your ships off and go home?"

"As fast as I can get my men aboard and out of here," said Grach Chai.

"Grach Chai."

"Yes?"

"You're hard and cruel but I don't think you're a liar."

"I'm not, Bryant."

Bryant lowered the weapon. "All right, go ahead. But remember this! We'll be coming into the Cloud someday!"

Grach Chai smiled. "Come ahead. You'll find Varkon waiting for you."

He turned and walked away out onto the red plain. Bryant looked at his receding figure, and looked down at his weapon, and smiled.

He waited. A little after noon there was a clap of distant thunder and then another, and two streaks of flame went up into the sky.

Bryant rose and began to walk toward the distant pylon. If the radio worked, he thought that help would get here in two days.

It was three, actually, before the ship from the nearest base far along the Rim lifted off the rusty planet into the glare of the red sun. Bryant, with Cyra at the port, looked at the world of his boyhood.

He thought of the men of Kothmar, under the buried dome, and of the Roving.

Dying dreamers—but also cosmic kings indeed, free of the wider universe that he would never see, lords of a million, million suns...

His arm tightened around Cyra. He did not think that he would ever forget the Roving.

He thought perhaps when he was old, and everything had changed, he might come back…

THE END

If you've enjoyed this book, you will not want to miss these terrific titles...

ARMCHAIR SCI-FI & HORROR DOUBLE NOVELS, $12.95 each

D-91 **THE TIME TRAP** by Henry Kuttner
THE LUNAR LICHEN by Hal Clement

D-92 **SARGASSO OF LOST STARSHIPS** by Poul Anderson
THE ICE QUEEN by Don Wilcox

D-93 **THE PRINCE OF SPACE** by Jack Williamson
POWER by Harl Vincent

D-94 **PLANET OF NO RETURN** by Howard Browne
THE ANNIHILATOR COMES by Ed Earl Repp

D-95 **THE SINISTER INVASION** by Edmond Hamilton
OPERATION TERROR by Murray Leinster

D-96 **TRANSIENT** by Ward Moore
THE WORLD-MOVER by George O. Smith

D-97 **FORTY DAYS HAS SEPTEMBER** by Milton Lesser
THE DEVIL'S PLANET by David Wright O'Brien

D-98 **THE CYBERENE** by Rog Phillips
BADGE OF INFAMY by Lester del Rey

D-99 **THE JUSTICE OF MARTIN BRAND** by Raymond A. Palmer
BRING BACK MY BRAIN by Dwight V. Swain

D-100 **WIDE-OPEN PLANET** by L. Sprague de Camp
AND THEN THE TOWN TOOK OFF by Richard Wilson

ARMCHAIR SCIENCE FICTION CLASSICS, $12.95 each

C-31 **THE GOLDEN GUARDSMEN**
by S. J. Byrne

C-32 **ONE AGAINST THE MOON**
by Donald A. Wollheim

C-33 **HIDDEN CITY**
by Chester S. Geier

ARMCHAIR SCI-FI & HORROR GEMS SERIES, $12.95 each

G-9 **SCIENCE FICTION GEMS, Vol. Five**
Clifford D. Simak and others

G-10 **HORROR GEMS, Vol. Five**
E. Hoffmann Price and others

If you've enjoyed this book, you will not want to miss these terrific titles...

ARMCHAIR SCI-FI & HORROR DOUBLE NOVELS, $12.95 each

D-101 **CONQUEST OF THE PLANETS** by John W. Campbell
THE MAN WHO ANNEXED THE MOON by Bob Olsen

D-102 **WEAPON FROM THE STARS** by Rog Phillips
THE EARTH WAR by Mack Reynolds

D-103 **THE ALIEN INTELLIGENCE** by Jack Williamson
INTO THE FOURTH DIMENSION by Ray Cummings

D-104 **THE CRYSTAL PLANETOIDS** by Stanton A. Coblentz
SURVIVORS FROM 9,000 B. C. by Robert Moore Williams

D-105 **THE TIME PROJECTOR** by David H. Keller, M.D. and David Lasser
STRANGE COMPULSION by Philip Jose Farmer

D-106 **WHOM THE GODS WOULD SLAY** by Paul W. Fairman
MEN IN THE WALLS by William Tenn

D-107 **LOCKED WORLDS** by Edmond Hamilton
THE LAND THAT TIME FORGOT by Edgar Rice Burroughs

D-108 **STAY OUT OF SPACE** by Dwight V. Swain
REBELS OF THE RED PLANET by Charles L. Fontenay

D-109 **THE METAMORPHS** by S. J. Byrne
MICROCOSMIC BUCCANEERS by Harl Vincent

D-110 **YOU CAN'T ESCAPE FROM MARS** by E. K. Jarvis
THE MAN WITH FIVE LIVES by David V. Reed

ARMCHAIR SCIENCE FICTION CLASSICS, $12.95 each

C-34 **30 DAY WONDER**
by Richard Wilson

C-35 **G.O.G. 666**
by John Taine

C-36 **RALPH 124C 41+**
by Hugo Gernsback

ARMCHAIR SCI-FI & HORROR GEMS SERIES, $12.95 each

G-11 **SCIENCE FICTION GEMS, Vol. Six**
Edmond Hamilton and others

G-12 **HORROR GEMS, Vol. Six**
H. P. Lovecraft and others

If you've enjoyed this book, you will not want to miss these terrific titles...

ARMCHAIR SCIENCE FICTION CLASSICS, $12.95 each

C-40 **MODEL FOR MURDER**
by Stephen Marlowe

C-41 **PRELUDE TO MURDER**
by Sterling Noel

C-42 **DEAD WEIGHT**
by Frank Kane

C-43 **A DAME CALLED MURDER**
by Milton Ozaki

C-44 **THE GREATEST ADVENTURE**
by John Taine

C-45 **THE EXILE OF TIME**
by Ray Cummings

C-46 **STORM OVER WARLOCK**
by Andre Norton

C-47 **MAN OF MANY MINDS**
by E. Everett Evans

C-48 **THE GODS OF MARS**
by Edgar Rice Burroughs

C-49 **BRIGANDS OF THE MOON**
by Ray Cummings

C-50 **SPACE HOUNDS OF IPC**
by E. E. "Doc" Smith

C-51 **THE LANI PEOPLE**
J. F. Bone

C-52 **THE MOON POOL**
by A. Merritt

C-53 **IN THE DAYS OF THE COMET**
by H. G. Wells

C-54 **TRIPLANETARY**
C. C. Doc Smith

If you've enjoyed this book, you will not want to miss these terrific titles…

ARMCHAIR SCI-FI & HORROR DOUBLE NOVELS, $12.95 each

D-121   **THE GENIUS BEASTS** by Frederik Pohl
          THIS WORLD IS TABOO by Murray Leinster

D-122   **THE COSMIC LOOTERS** by Edmond Hamilton
          WANDL THE INVADER by Ray Cummings

D-123   **ROBOT MEN OF BUBBLE CITY** by Rog Phillips
          DRAGON ARMY by William Morrison

D-124   **LAND BEYOND THE LENS** by S. J. Byrne
          DIPLOMAT-AT-ARMS by Keith Laumer

D-125   **VOYAGE OF THE ASTEROID, THE** by Laurence Manning
          REVOLT OF THE OUTWORLDS by Milton Lesser

D-126   **OUTLAW IN THE SKY** by Chester S. Geier
          LEGACY FROM MARS by Raymond Z. Gallun

D-127   **THE GREAT FLYING SAUCER INVASION** by Geoff St. Reynard
          THE BIG TIME by Fritz Leiber

D-128   **MIRAGE FOR PLANET X** by Stanley Mullen
          POLICE YOUR PLANET by Lester del Rey

D-129   **THE BRAIN SINNER** by Alan E. Nourse
          DEATH FROM THE SKIES by A. Hyatt Verrill

D-130   **CRY CHAOS** by Dwight V. Swain
          THE DOOR THROUGH SPACE By Marion Zimmer Bradley

ARMCHAIR SCIENCE FICTION CLASSICS, $12.95 each

C-55   **UNDER THE TRIPLE SUNS**
        by Stanton A. Coblentz (single) 1950s, Fantasy Press

C-56   **STONE FROM THE GREEN STAR**
        by Jack Williamson, Amazing 10 & 11/31, (cleared by Eli)

C-57   **ALIEN MINDS**
        by E. Everett Evans

ARMCHAIR SCI-FI & HORROR GEMS SERIES, $12.95 each

G-13   **SCIENCE FICTION GEMS, Vol. Seven**
        Jack Vance and others

G-14   **HORROR GEMS, Vol. Seven**
        Robert Bloch and others

If you've enjoyed this book, you will not want to miss these terrific titles...

ARMCHAIR SCI-FI & HORROR DOUBLE NOVELS, $12.95 each

D-131 **COSMIC KILL** by Robert Silverberg
BEYOND THE END OF SPACE by John W. Campbell

D-132 **THE DARK OTHER** by Stanley Weinbaum)
WITCH OF THE DEMON SEAS by Poul Anderson

D-133 **PLANET OF THE SMALL MEN** by Murray Leinster
MASTERS OF SPACE by E. E. "Doc" Smith & E. Everett Evans

D-134 **BEFORE THE ASTEROIDS** by Harl Vincent
SIXTH GLACIER, THE by Marius

D-135 **AFTER WORLD'S END** by Jack Williamson
THE FLOATING ROBOT by David Wright O'Brien

D-136 **NINE WORLDS WEST** by Paul W. Fairman
FRONTIERS BEYOND THE SUN by Rog Phillips

D-137 **THE COSMIC KINGS** by Edmond Hamilton
LONE STAR PLANET by H. Beam Piper & John J. McGuire

D-138 **BEYOND THE DARKNESS** by S. J. Byrne
THE FIRELESS AGE by David H. Keller, M. D.

D-139 **FLAME JEWEL OF THE ANCIENTS** by Edwin L. Graber
THE PIRATE PLANET by Charles W. Diffin

D-140 **ADDRESS: CENTAURI** by F. L. Wallace
IF THESE BE GODS by Algis Budrys

ARMCHAIR SCIENCE FICTION & HORROR CLASSICS, $12.95 each

C-58 **THE WITCHING NIGHT**
by Leslie Waller

C-59 **SEARCH THE SKY**
by Frederick Pohl and C. M. Kornbluth

C-60 **INTRIGUE ON THE UPPER LEVEL**
by Thomas Tempel Hoyne

ARMCHAIR SCI-FI & HORROR GEMS SERIES, $12.95 each

G-15 **SCIENCE FICTION GEMS, Vol. Eight**
Keith Laumer and others

G-16 **HORROR GEMS, Vol. Eight**
Algernon Blackwood and others

THEY MOVED THE ALAMO TO THE STARS—AND DEFIED ALL SPACE!

The name of the planet was New Texas; the by-word of the people was independence, so the citizens of this maverick planet fought against the protective ties of the Solar League.

And for Stephen Silk, League ambassador to New Texas, the job was twofold. Getting that pistol-packing populace to admit that they needed anyone's protection would have been a tough enough task in itself. But add to it the fact that Silk realized New Texas—as well as the rest of the galaxy—was in danger of a z'Srauff attack, and the job became impossible. It was pretty common knowledge that the z'Srauff were a race evolved from canine-like ancestors—and there wasn't a Texan alive who could be scared by a talkin' dawg!

But if Silk couldn't get them to act, and fast, there wasn't going to be a Texan alive, scared or otherwise. The whole universe would be going to the dogs!

CAST OF CHARACTERS

AMBASSADOR STEPHEN SILK
Even with the veil of diplomatic immunity, he was still going to need a bullet-proof vest!

COLONEL ANDREW JACKSON HICKOCK
He excelled in a most unusual game of chance—widely known as New Texan Politics.

AMBASSADOR GGLAFRR VUVUVU
This diplomat's name was almost unpronounceable and his bark was much milder than his bite.

KETTLE-BELLY SAM BONNEY
As the residing mayor of Bonneyville, New Texas, he had a crooked path to follow!

HODDY RINGO
He was the only bodyguard on New Texas who needed his employer's protection.

JUDGE NELSON
When he pounded his gavel, all he got was a good dose of mayhem.

LONE STAR
PLANET

By
H. BEAM PIPER & JOHN J. McGUIRE

ARMCHAIR FICTION
PO Box 4369, Medford, Oregon 97504

CHAPTER ONE

They started giving me the business as soon as I came through the door into the Secretary's outer office.

There was Ethel K'wang-Li, the Secretary's receptionist, at her desk. There was Courtlant Staynes, the assistant secretary to the Undersecretary for Economic Penetration, and Norman Gazarin, from Protocol, and Toby Lawder, from Humanoid Peoples' Affairs, and Raoul Chavier, and Hans Mannteufel, and Olga Reznik.

It was a wonder there weren't more of them watching the condemned man's march to the gibbet: the word that the Secretary had called me in must have gotten all over the Department since the offices had opened.

"Ah, Mr. Machiavelli, I presume," Ethel kicked off.

"Machiavelli, Junior." Olga picked up the ball. "At least, that's the way he signs it."

"God's gift to the Consular Service, and the Consular Service's gift to Policy Planning," Gazarin added.

"Take it easy, folks. These Hooligan Diplomats would as soon shoot you as look at you," Mannteufel warned.

"Be sure and tell the Secretary that your friends all want important posts in the Galactic Empire." Olga again.

"Well, I'm glad some of you could read it," I fired back. "Maybe even a few of you understood what it was all about."

"Don't worry, Silk," Gazarin told me. "Secretary Ghopal understands what it was all about. All too well, you'll find."

A buzzer sounded gently on Ethel K'wang-Li's desk. She snatched up the handphone and whispered into it. A deathly silence filled the room while she listened, whispered some more, then hung it up.

They were all staring at me.

"Secretary Ghopal is ready to see Mr. Stephen Silk," she said. "This way, please."

As I started across the room, Staynes began drumming on the top of the desk with his fingers, the slow reiterated rhythm to which a man marches to a military execution.

"A cigarette?" Lawder inquired tonelessly. "A glass of rum?"

THERE were three men in the Secretary of State's private office. Ghopal Singh, the Secretary, dark-faced, gray-haired, slender and elegant, meeting me halfway to his desk. Another slender man, in black, with a silver-threaded, black neck-scarf: Rudolf Klüng, the Secretary of the Department of Aggression.

And a huge, gross-bodied man with a fat baby-face and opaque black eyes.

When I saw him, I really began to get frightened.

The fat man was Natalenko, the Security Coördinator.

"Good morning, Mister Silk," Secretary Ghopal greeted me, his hand extended. "Gentlemen, Mr. Stephen Silk, about whom we were speaking. This way, Mr. Silk, if you please."

There was a low coffee-table at the rear of the office, and four easy chairs around it. On the round brass table-top were cups and saucers, a coffee urn, cigarettes—and a copy of the current issue of the *Galactic Statesmen's Journal*, open at an article entitled *Probable Future Courses of Solar*

League Diplomacy, by somebody who had signed himself Machiavelli, Jr.

I was beginning to wish that the pseudonymous Machiavelli, Jr. had never been born, or, at least, had stayed on Theta Virgo IV and been a wineberry planter as his father had wanted him to be.

As I sat down and accepted a cup of coffee, I avoided looking at the periodical. They were probably going to hang it around my neck before they shoved me out of the airlock.

"Mr. Silk is, as you know, in our Consular Service," Ghopal was saying to the others. "Back on Luna on rotation, doing something in Mr. Halvord's section. He is the gentleman who did such a splendid job for us on Assha—Gamma Norma III.

"And, as he has just demonstrated," he added, gesturing toward the *Statesman's Journal* on the Benares-work table, "he is a student both of the diplomacy of the past and the implications of our present policies."

"A bit frank," Klüng commented dubiously.

"But judicious," Natalenko squeaked, in the high eunuchoid voice that came so incongruously from his bulk. "He aired his singularly accurate predictions in a periodical that doesn't have a circulation of more than a thousand copies outside his own department. And I don't think the public's semantic reactions to the terminology of imperialism is as bad as you imagine. They seem quite satisfied, now, with the change in the title of your department, from Defense to Aggression."

"Well, we've gone into that, gentlemen," Ghopal said. "If the article really makes trouble for us, we can always disavow it. There's no censorship of the *Journal*. And Mr. Silk won't be around to draw fire on us."

Here it comes, I thought.

"That sounds pretty ominous, doesn't it, Mr. Silk?" Natalenko tittered happily, like a ten-year-old who has just found a new beetle to pull the legs out of.

"It's really not as bad as it sounds, Mr. Silk," Ghopal hastened to reassure me. "We are going to have to banish you for a while, but I daresay that won't be so bad. The social life here on Luna has probably begun to pall, anyhow. So we're sending you to Capella IV."

"Capella IV," I repeated, trying to remember something about it. Capella was a GO-type, like Sol; that wouldn't be so bad.

"New Texas," Klüng helped me out.

Oh, God, no! I thought.

"It happens that we need somebody of your sort on that planet, Mr. Silk," Ghopal said. "Some of the trouble is in my department and some of it is in Mr. Klüng's; for that reason, perhaps it would be better if Coördinator Natalenko explained it to you."

"You know, I assume, our chief interest in New Texas?" Natalenko asked.

"I had some of it for breakfast, sir," I replied. "Supercow."

Natalenko tittered again. "Yes, New Texas is the butcher shop of the galaxy. In more ways than one, I'm afraid you'll find. They just butchered one of our people there a short while ago. Our Ambassador, in fact."

That would be Silas Cumshaw, and this was the first I'd heard about it.

I asked when it had happened.

"A couple of months ago. We just heard about it last evening, when the news came in on a freighter from there. Which serves to point up something you stressed in your article—the difficulties of trying to run a centralized democratic government on a galactic scale. But we have another interest, which may be even more urgent than our need for New Texan meat. You've heard, of course, of the z'Srauff."

That was a statement, not a question; Natalenko wasn't trying to insult me. I knew who the z'Srauff were; I'd run into them, here and there. One of the extra-solar intelligent humanoid races, who seemed to have been evolved from canine or canine-like ancestors, instead of primates. Most of them could speak Basic English, but I never saw one who would admit to understanding more of our language than the 850-word Basic vocabulary. They occupied a half-dozen planets in a small star-cluster about forty light-years beyond the Capella system. They had developed normal-space reaction-drive ships before we came into contact with them, and they had quickly picked up the hyperspace-drive from us back in those days when the Solar League was still playing Missionaries of Progress and trying to run a galaxy-wide Point-Four program.

In the past century, it had become almost impossible for anybody to get into their star-group, although z'Srauff ships were orbiting in on every planet that the League had settled or controlled. There were z'Srauff traders and small merchants all over the galaxy, and you almost never saw one of them without a camera. Their little meteor-mining boats were everywhere, and all of them carried more of the most modern radar and astrogational equipment than a meteor-miner's lifetime earnings would pay for.

I also knew that they were one of the chief causes of ulcers and premature gray hair at the League capital on Luna. I'd done a little reading on pre-spaceflight Terran history; I had been impressed by the parallel between the present situation and one which had culminated, two and a half centuries before, on the morning of 7 December, 1941.

"What," Natalenko inquired, "do you think Machiavelli, Junior would do about the z'Srauff?"

"We have a Department of Aggression," I replied. "Its mottoes are, 'Stop trouble before it starts,' and, 'If we have to fight, let's do it on the other fellow's real estate.' But this situation is just a little too delicate for literal application of those principles. An unprovoked attack on the z'Srauff would set every other non-human race in the galaxy against us... Would an attack by the z'Srauff on New Texas constitute just provocation?"

"It might. New Texas is an independent planet. Its people are descendants of emigrants from Terra who wanted to get away from the rule of the Solar League. We've been trying for half a century to persuade the New Texan government to join the League. We need their planet, for both strategic and commercial reasons. With the z'Srauff for neighbors, they need us as much at least as we need them. The problem is to make them understand that."

I nodded again. "And an attack by the z'Srauff would do that, too, sir," I said.

Natalenko tittered again. "You see, gentlemen! Our Mr. Silk picks things up very handily, doesn't he?" He turned to Secretary of State Ghopal. "You take it from there," he invited.

Ghopal Singh smiled benignly. "Well, that's it, Stephen," he said. "We need a man on New Texas who can get things done. Three things, to be exact.

"First, find out why poor Mr. Cumshaw was murdered, and what can be done about it to maintain our prestige without alienating the New Texans.

"Second, bring the government and people of New Texas to a realization that they need the Solar League as much as we need them.

"And, third, forestall or expose the plans for the z'Srauff invasion of New Texas."

Is that all, now? I thought. *He doesn't want a diplomat; he wants a magician.*

"And what," I asked, "will my official position be on New Texas, sir? Or will I have one, of any sort?"

"Oh, yes, indeed, Mr. Silk. Your official position will be that of Ambassador Plenipotentiary and Envoy Extraordinary. That, I believe, is the only vacancy which exists in the Diplomatic Service on that planet."

At Dumbarton Oaks Diplomatic Academy, they haze the freshmen by making them sit on a one-legged stool and balance a teacup and saucer on one knee while the upper classmen pelt them with ping-pong balls. Whoever invented that and the other similar forms of hazing was one of the great geniuses of the Service. So I sipped my coffee, set down the cup, took a puff from my cigarette, then said:

"I am indeed deeply honored, Mr. Secretary. I trust I needn't go into any assurances that I will do everything possible to justify your trust in me."

"I believe he will, Mr. Secretary," Natalenko piped, in a manner that chilled my blood.

"Yes, I believe so," Ghopal Singh said. "Now, Mr. Ambassador, there's a liner in orbit two thousand miles off Luna, which has been held from blasting off for the last eight hours, waiting for you. Don't bother packing more than a few things; you can get everything you'll need aboard, or at New Austin, the planetary capital. We have a man whom Coördinator Natalenko has secured for us, a native New Texan, Hoddy Ringo by name. He'll act as your personal secretary. He's aboard the ship now. You'll have to hurry, I'm afraid... Well, *bon voyage*, Mr. Ambassador."

CHAPTER TWO

The death-watch outside had grown to about fifteen or twenty. They were all waiting in happy anticipation as I came out of the Secretary's office.

"What did he do to you, Silk?" Courtlant Staynes asked, amusedly.

"Demoted me. Kicked me off the Hooligan Diplomats," I said glumly.

"Demoted you from the Consular Service?" Staynes asked scornfully. "Impossible!"

"Yes. He demoted me to the Cookie Pushers. Clear down to Ambassador."

They got a terrific laugh. I went out, wondering what sort of noises they'd make, the next morning, when the appointments sheet was posted.

I GATHERED a few things together, mostly small personal items, and all the microfilms that I could find on New Texas, then got aboard the Space Navy cutter that was waiting to take me to the ship. It was a four-hour trip and I put in the time going over my hastily-assembled microfilm library and using a stenophone to dictate a reading list for the spacetrip.

As I rolled up the stenophone-tape, I wondered what sort of secretary they had given me; and, in passing, why Natalenko's department had furnished him.

Hoddy Ringo...

Queer name, but in a galactic civilization, you find all sorts of names and all sorts of people bearing them, so I was prepared for anything.

And I found it.

I found him standing with the ship's captain, inside the airlock, when I boarded the big, spherical space-liner. A tubby little man, with shoulders and arms he had never developed doing secretarial work, and a good-natured, not particularly intelligent face.

See the happy moron, he doesn't give a damn, I thought.

Then I took a second look at him. He might be happy, but he wasn't a moron. He just looked like one. Natalenko's people often did, as one of their professional assets.

I also noticed that he had a bulge under his left armpit the size of an eleven-mm army automatic.

He was, I'd been told, a native of New Texas. I gathered, after talking with him for a while, that he had been away from his home planet for over five years, was glad to be going back, and especially glad that he was going back under the protection of Solar League diplomatic immunity.

In fact, I rather got the impression that, without such protection, he wouldn't have been going back at all.

I made another discovery. My personal secretary, it seemed, couldn't read stenotype. I found that out when I gave him the tape I'd dictated aboard the cutter, to transcribe for me.

"Gosh, boss. I can't make anything out of this stuff," he confessed, looking at the combination shorthand-Braille that my voice had put onto the tape.

"Well, then, put it in a player and transcribe it by ear," I told him.

He didn't seem to realize that that could be done.

"How did you come to be sent as my secretary, if you can't do secretarial work?" I wanted to know.

He got out a bag of tobacco and a book of papers and began rolling a cigarette, with one hand.

"Why, shucks, boss, nobody seemed to think I'd have to do this kinda work," he said. "I was just sent along to show you the way around New Texas, and see you don't get inta no trouble."

He got his handmade cigarette drawing, and hitched the strap that went across his back and looped under his right arm. "A guy that don't know the way around can get inta a lotta trouble on New Texas. If you call gettin' killed trouble."

So he was a bodyguard...and I wondered what else he was. One thing, it would take him forty-two years to send a radio message back to Luna, and I could keep track of any other messages he sent, in letters or on tape, by ships. In the end, I transcribed my own tape, and settled down to laying out my three weeks' study-course on my new post.

I found, however, that the whole thing could be learned in a few hours. The rest of what I had was duplication, some of it contradictory, and it all boiled down to this:

Capella IV had been settled during the first wave of extrasolar colonization, after the Fourth World—or First Interplanetary—War. Some time around 2100. The settlers had come from a place in North America called Texas, one of the old United States. They had a lengthy history—independent republic, admission to the United States, secession from the United States, reconquest by the United States, and general intransigence under the United States, the United Nations and the Solar League. When the laws of non-Einsteinian physics were discovered and the hyperspace-drive was developed, practically the entire population of Texas had taken to space to find a new home and independence from everybody.

They had found Capella IV, a Terra-type planet, with a slightly higher mean temperature, a lower mass and lower gravitational field, about one-quarter water and three-quarters land-surface, at a stage of evolutionary development approximately that of Terra during the late Pliocene. They also found supercow, a big mammal looking like the unsuccessful attempt of a hippopotamus to impersonate a dachshund and about the size of a nuclear-steam locomotive. On New Texas' plains, there were billions of them; their meat fit for the gods of Olympus. So New Texas had become the meat-supplier to the galaxy.

There was little in any of the microfilm-books about the politics in New Texas and what was there was scornful. There were such expressions as 'anarchy tempered by assassination,' and 'grotesque parody of democracy.'

There would, I assumed, be more exact information in the material which had been shoved into my hand just before boarding the cutter from Luna, in a package labeled *TOP SECRET: TO BE OPENED ONLY IN SPACE, AFTER THE FIRST HYPERJUMP.* There was also a big trunk that had been placed in my suite, sealed and bearing the same instructions.

I got Hoddy out of the suite as soon as the ship had passed out of the normal space-time continuum, locked the door of my cabin and opened the parcel.

It contained only two loose-leaf notebooks, both labeled with the Solar League and Department seals, both adorned with the customary bloodthirsty threats against the unauthorized and the indiscreet. They were numbered *ONE* and *TWO*.

ONE contained four pages. On the first, I read:

FINAL MESSAGE OF THE FIRST
SOLAR LEAGUE AMBASSADOR TO
NEW TEXAS
ANDREW JACKSON HICKOCK

I agree with none of the so-called information about this planet on file with the State Department on Luna. The people of New Texas are certainly not uncouth barbarians. Their manners and customs, while lively and unconventional, are most charming. Their dress is graceful and practical, not grotesque; their soft speech is pleasing to the ear. Their flag is the original flag of the Republic of Texas; it is definitely not a barbaric travesty of our own emblem. And the underlying premises of their political system should, as far as possible, be incorporated into the organization of the Solar League. Here politics is an exciting and exacting game, in which only the true representative of all the people can survive.

DEPARTMENT ADDENDUM

After five years on New Texas, Andrew Jackson Hickock resigned, married a daughter of a local rancher and became a naturalized citizen of that planet. He is still active in politics there, often in opposition to Solar League policies.

That didn't sound like too bad an advertisement for the planet. I was even feeling cheerful when I turned to the next page, and:

FINAL MESSAGE OF THE SECOND
SOLAR LEAGUE AMBASSADOR TO
NEW TEXAS
CYRIL GODWINSON

Yes and no; perhaps and perhaps not; pardon me; I agree with everything you say. Yes and no; perhaps and perhaps not; pardon me; I agree...

DEPARTMENT ADDENDUM
After seven years on New Texas, Ambassador Godwinson was recalled; adjudged hopelessly insane.

And then:

FINAL MESSAGE OF THE THIRD
SOLAR LEAGUE AMBASSADOR TO
NEW TEXAS
R. F. GULLIS
I find it very pleasant to inform you that when you are reading this, I will be dead.

DEPARTMENT ADDENDUM
Committed suicide after six months on New Texas.

I turned to the last page cautiously, found:

FINAL MESSAGE OF THE FOURTH
SOLAR LEAGUE AMBASSADOR TO
NEW TEXAS
SILAS CUMSHAW
I came to this planet ten years ago as a man of pronounced and outspoken convictions. I have managed to keep myself alive here by becoming an inoffensive nonentity. If I continue in this course, it will be only at the cost of my self-respect. Beginning tonight, I am going to state and maintain positive opinions on the relation between this planet and the Solar League.

DEPARTMENT ADDENDUM
Murdered at the home of Andrew J. Hickock. (see p. 1.)

And that was the end of the first notebook. Nice, cheerful reading; complete, solid briefing.

I was, frankly, almost afraid to open the second notebook. I hefted it cautiously at first, saw that it contained only about as many pages as the first and that those pages were sealed with a band around them.

I took a quick peek, read the words on the band:

Before reading, open the sealed trunk which has been included with your luggage.

So I laid aside the book and dragged out the sealed trunk, hesitated, then opened it.

Nothing shocked me more than to find the trunk...full of clothes.

There were four pairs of trousers, light blue, dark blue, gray and black, with wide cuffs at the bottoms. There were six or eight shirts, their colors running the entire spectrum in the most violent shades. There were a couple of vests. There were two pairs of short boots with high heels and fancy leather-working, and a couple of hats with four-inch brims.

And there was a wide leather belt, practically a leather corset.

I stared at the belt, wondering if I was really seeing what was in front of me.

Attached to the belt were a pair of pistols in right- and left-hand holsters. The pistols were seven-mm Krupp-Tatta Ultraspeed automatics, and the holsters were the spring-ejection, quick-draw holsters which were the secret of the State Department Special Services.

This must be a mistake, I thought. *I'm an Ambassador now and Ambassadors never carry weapons.*

The sanctity of an Ambassador's person not only made the carrying of weapons unnecessary, so that an armed Ambassador was a contradiction of diplomatic terms, but it would be an outrageous insult to the nation to which he had been accredited.

Like taking a poison-taster to a friendly dinner.

Maybe I was supposed to give the belt and the holsters to Hoddy Ringo...

So I tore the sealed band off the second notebook and read through it.

I was to wear the local costume on New Texas. That was something unusual; even in the Hooligan Diplomats, we leaned over backward in wearing Terran costume to distinguish ourselves from the people among whom we worked.

I was further advised to start wearing the high boots immediately, on shipboard, to accustom myself to the heels. These, I was informed, were traditional. They had served a useful purpose, in the early days on Terran Texas, when all travel had been on horseback. On horseless and mechanized New Texas, they were a useless but venerated part of the cultural heritage.

There were bits of advice about the hat, and the trousers, which for some obscure reason were known as Levis. And I was informed, as an order, that I was to wear the belt and the pistols at all times outside the Embassy itself.

That was all of the second notebook.

The two notebooks, plus my conversation with Ghopal, Klüng and Natalenko, completed my briefing for my new post.

I slid off my shoes and pulled on a pair of boots. They fitted perfectly. Evidently I had been tapped for this job as soon as word of Silas Cumshaw's death had reached Luna and there must have been some fantastic hurrying to get my outfit ready.

I didn't like that any too well, and I liked the order to carry the pistols even less. Not that I had any objection to carrying weapons, *per se*: I had been born and raised on Theta Virgo IV, where the children aren't allowed outside the house unattended until they've learned to shoot.

But I did have strenuous objections to being sent, virtually ignorant of local customs, on a mission where I was ordered to commit deliberate provocation of the local government, immediately on the heels of my predecessor's violent death.

The author of *Probable Future Courses of Solar League Diplomacy* had recommended the use of provocation to justify conquest. If the New Texans murdered two Solar League Ambassadors in a row, nobody would blame the League for moving in with a space-fleet and an army…

I was beginning to understand how Doctor Guillotin must have felt while his neck was being shoved into his own invention.

I looked again at the notebooks, each marked in red: *Familiarize yourself with contents and burn or disintegrate.*

I'd have to do that, of course. There were a few non-humans and a lot of non-League people aboard this ship. I couldn't let any of them find out what we considered a full briefing for a new Ambassador.

So I wrapped them in the original package and went down to the lower passenger zone, where I found the ship's third officer. I told him that I had some secret diplomatic matter to be destroyed and he took me to the engine room. I shoved the package into one of the mass-energy convertors and watched it resolve itself into its constituent protons, neutrons and electrons.

On the way back, I stopped in at the ship's bar.

Hoddy Ringo was there, wrapped up in—and I use the words literally—a young lady from the Alderbaran system. She was on her way home from one of the quickie divorce courts on Terra and was celebrating her marital emancipation. They were so entangled with each other that they didn't notice me. When they left the bar, I slipped after them until I saw them enter the lady's stateroom. That, of course, would have Hoddy immobilized—better word, located—for a while. So I went back to our suite, picked the lock of Hoddy's room, and allowed myself half an hour to search his luggage.

All of his clothes were new, but there were not a great many of them. Evidently he was planning to re-outfit himself on New Texas. There were a few odds and ends, the kind any man with a real home planet will hold on to, in the luggage.

He had another eleven-mm pistol, made by Consolidated-Martian Metalworks, mate to the one he was carrying in a shoulder-holster, and a wide two-holster belt like the one furnished me, but quite old.

I greeted the sight and the meaning of the old holsters with joy: they weren't the State Department Special Services type. That meant that Hoddy was just one of Natalenko's run-of-the-gallows cutthroats, not important enough to be issued the secret equipment.

But I was a little worried over what I found hidden in the lining of one of his bags, a letter neatly addressed to Space-Commander Lucius C. Stonehenge, Aggression Department Attaché, New Austin Embassy. I didn't have either the time or the equipment to open it. But, knowing our various Departments, I tried to reassure myself with the thought that it was only a letter-of-credence, with the real message to be delivered orally.

About the real message I had no doubts: *arrange the murder of Ambassador Stephen Silk in such a way that it looks like another New Texan job...*

STARTING that evening—or what passed for evening aboard a ship in hyperspace—Hoddy and I began a positively epochal binge together.

I had it figured this way: as long as we were on board ship, I was perfectly safe. On the ship, in fact, Hoddy would definitely have given his life to save mine. I'd have to be killed on New Texas to give Klüng's boys their excuse for moving in.

And there was always the chance, with no chance too slender for me to ignore, that I might be able to get Hoddy drunk enough to talk, yet still be sober enough myself to remember what he said.

Exact times, details, faces, names, came to me through a sort of hazy blur as Hoddy and I drank something he called superbourbon—a New Texan drink that Bourbon County, Kentucky, would never have recognized. They had no corn on New Texas. This stuff was made out of something called superyams.

There were at least two things I got out of the binge. First, I learned to slug down the national drink without batting an eye. Second, I learned to control my expression as I uncovered the fact that everything on New Texas was supersomething.

I was also cautious enough, before we really got started, to leave my belt and guns with the purser. I didn't want

Hoddy poking around those secret holsters. And I remember telling the captain to radio New Austin as soon as we came out of our last hyperspace-jump, then to send the ship's doctor around to give me my hangover treatments.

But the one thing I wanted to remember, as the hangover shots brought me back to normal life, I found was the one thing I couldn't remember. What was the name of that girl—a big, beautiful blond—who joined the party along with Hoddy's grass widow from Alderbaran and stayed with it to the end?

Damn, I wished I could remember her name!

WHEN we were fifteen thousand miles off-planet and the lighters from New Austin spaceport were reported on the way, I got into the skin-tight Levis, the cataclysmic-colored shirt, and the loose vest, tucked my big hat under my arm, and went to the purser's office for my guns, buckling them on. When I got back to the suite, Hoddy had put on his pistols and was practicing quick draws in front of the mirror. He took one look at my armament and groaned.

"You're gonna get yourself killed for sure, with that rig, an' them popguns," he told me.

"These popguns'll shoot harder and make bigger holes than that pair of museum-pieces you're carrying," I replied.

"An' them holsters!" Hoddy continued. "Why, it'd take all day to get your guns outa them! You better let me find you a real rig, when we get to New Austin…"

There was a chance, of course, that he knew what I was using and wanted to hide his knowledge. I doubted that.

"Sure, you State Department guys always know everything," he went on. "Like them microfilm-books you was readin'. I try to tell you what things is really like on New Texas, an' you let it go in one ear an' out the other."

Then he wandered off to say good-bye to the grass widow from Alderbaran, leaving me to make the last-minute check on the luggage. I was hoping I'd be able to see that blond...what *was* her name; Gail something-or-other. Let's see, she'd been at some Terran university, and she was on her way home to...to New Texas! Of course!

I SAW her, half an hour later, in the crowd around the airlock when the lighters came alongside, and I tried to push my way toward her. As I did, the airlock opened, the crowd surged toward it, and she was carried along. Then the airlock closed, after she had passed through and before I could get to it. That meant I'd have to wait for the second lighter.

So I made the best of it, and spent the next half-hour watching the disc of the planet grow into a huge ball that filled the lower half of the viewscreen and then lose its curvature, and instead of moving in toward the planet, we were going down toward it.

CHAPTER THREE

New Austin spaceport was a huge place, a good fifty miles outside the city. As we descended, I could see that it was laid out like a wheel, with the landings and the blast-off stands around the hub, and high buildings—packing houses and refrigeration plants—along the many spokes. It showed a technological level quite out of keeping with the accounts I had read, or the stories Hoddy had told, about the simple ranch life of the planet. Might be foreign capital invested there, and I made a mental note to find out whose.

On the other hand, Old Texas, on Terra, had been heavily industrialized; so much so that the state itself could handle the gigantic project of building enough spaceships to move almost the whole population into space.

Then the landing-field was rushing up at us, with the nearer ends of the roadways and streets drawing close and the far ends lengthening out away from us. The other lighter was already down, and I could see a crowd around it.

There was a crowd waiting for us when we got out and went down the escalators to the ground, and as I had expected, a special group of men waiting for me. They were headed by a tall, slender individual in the short black Eisenhower jacket, gray-striped trousers and black homburg that was the uniform of the Diplomatic Service, alias the Cookie Pushers.

Over their heads at the other rocket-boat, I could see the gold-gleaming head of the girl I'd met on the ship.

I tried to push through the crowd and get to her. As I did, the Cookie Pusher got in my way.

"Mr. Silk! Mr. Ambassador! Here we are!" he was clamoring. "The car for the Embassy is right over here!" He clutched my elbow. "You have no idea how glad we all are to see you, Mr. Ambassador!"

"Yes, yes; of course. Now, there's somebody over there I have to see, at once." I tried to pull myself loose from his grasp.

Across the concrete between the two lighters, I could see the girl push out of the crowd around her and wave a hand to me. I tried to yell to her; but just then another lighter, loaded with freight, started to lift out at another nearby stand, with the roar of half a dozen Niagaras. The thin man in the striped trousers added to the uproar by shouting into my ear and pulling at me.

"We haven't time!" he finally managed to make himself heard. "We're dreadfully late now, sir! You must come with us."

Hoddy, too, had caught hold of me by the other arm.

"Come on, boss. There's gotta be some reason why he's got himself in an uproar about whatever it is. You'll see her again."

Then, the whole gang—Hoddy, the thin man with the black homburg, his younger accomplice in identical garb, and the chauffeur—all closed in on me and pushed me, pulled me, half-carried me, fifty yards across the concrete to where their air-car was parked. By this time, the tall blond had gotten clear of the mob around her and was waving frantically at me. I tried to wave back, but I was literally crammed into the car and flung down on the seat.

At the same time, the chauffeur was jumping in, extending the car's wings, jetting up.

"Great God!" I bellowed. "This is the damnedest piece of impudence I've ever had to suffer from any subordinates in my whole State Department experience! I want an explanation out of you, and it'd better be a good one!"

There was a deafening silence in the car for a moment. The thin man moved himself off my lap, then sat there looking at me with the heartbroken eyes of a friendly dog that had just been kicked for something which wasn't really its fault.

"Mr. Ambassador, you can't imagine how sorry we all are, but if we hadn't gotten you away from the spaceport and to the Embassy at once, we would all have been much sorrier."

"Somebody here gunnin' for the Ambassador?" Hoddy demanded sharply.

"Oh, no! I hadn't even thought of that," the thin man almost gibbered. "But your presence at the Embassy is of immediate and urgent necessity. You have no idea of the state into which things have gotten… Oh, pardon me, Mr. Ambassador. I am Gilbert W. Thrombley, your chargé d'affaires." I shook hands with him. "And Mr. Benito Gomez, the Secretary of the Embassy." I shook hands with him, too, and started to introduce Mr. Hoddy Ringo.

Hoddy, however, had turned to look out the rear window; immediately, he gave a yelp.

"We got a tail, boss! Two of them! Look back there!"

There were two black eight-passenger aircars, of the same model, whizzing after us, making an obvious effort to overtake us. The chauffeur cursed and fired his auxiliary jets, then his rocket-booster.

Immediately, black rocket-fuel puffs shot away from the pursuing aircars.

Hoddy turned in his seat, cranked open a porthole-slit in the window, and poked one of his eleven-mm's out, letting the whole clip go. Thrombley and Gomez slid down onto the floor, and both began trying to drag me down with them, imploring me not to expose myself.

As far as I could see, there was nothing to expose myself to. The other cars kept coming, but neither of them were firing at us. There was also no indication that Hoddy's salvo had had any effect on them. Our chauffeur went into a perfect frenzy of twisting and dodging, at the same time using his radiophone to tell somebody to get the goddamn gate open in a hurry. I saw the blue skies and green plains of New Texas replacing one another above, under, in front of and behind us. Then the car set down on a broad stretch of concrete, the wings were retracted, and we went whizzing down a city street.

We whizzed down a number of streets. We cut corners on two wheels, and on one wheel, and, I was prepared to swear, on no wheels. A couple of times, with the wings retracted, we actually jetted into the air and jumped over vehicles in front of us, landing again with bone-shaking jolts. Then we made an abrupt turn and shot in under a concrete arch, and a big door banged shut behind us, and we stopped, in the middle of a wide patio, the front of the car a few inches short of a fountain. Four or five people, in diplomatic striped trousers, local dress and the uniform of the Space Marines, came running over.

Thrombley pulled himself erect and half-climbed, half-fell, out of the car. Gomez got out on the other side with Hoddy; I climbed out after Thrombley.

A tall, sandy-haired man in the uniform of the Space Navy came over.

"What the devil's the matter, Thrombley?" he demanded. Then, seeing me, he gave me as much of a salute as a naval officer will ever bestow on anybody in civilian clothes.

"Mr. Silk?" He looked at my costume and the pistols on my belt in well-bred concealment of surprise. "I'm your military attaché, Stonehenge; Space-Commander, Space Navy."

I noticed that Hoddy's ears had pricked up, but he wasn't making any effort to attract Stonehenge's attention. I shook hands with him, introduced Hoddy, and offered my cigarette case around.

"You seem to have had a hectic trip from the spaceport, Mr. Ambassador. What happened?"

Thrombley began accusing our driver of trying to murder the lot of us. Hoddy brushed him aside and explained:

"Just after we'd took off, two other cars took off after us. We speeded up, and they speeded up, too. Then your fly-boy, here, got fancy. That shook 'em off. Time we got into the city, we'd dropped them. Nice job of driving. Probably saved our lives."

"Shucks, that wasn't nothin'," the driver disclaimed. "When you drive for politicians, you're either good or you're good and dead."

"I'm surprised they started so soon," Stonehenge said. Then he looked around at my fellow-passengers, who seemed to have realized, by now, that they were no longer dangling by their fingernails over the brink of the grave. "But gentlemen, let's not keep the Ambassador standing out here in the hot sun."

So we went over the arches at the side of the patio, and were about to sit down when one of the Embassy servants came up, followed by a man in a loose vest and blue Levis and a big hat. He had a pair of automatics in his belt, too.

"I'm Captain Nelson; New Texas Rangers," he introduced himself. "Which one of you-all is Mr. Stephen Silk?"

I admitted it.

The Ranger pushed back his wide hat and grinned at me.

"I just can't figure this out," he said. "You're in the right place and the right company, but we got a report, from a mighty good source, that you'd been kidnapped at the spaceport by a gang of thugs!"

"A blond source?" I made curving motions with my hands. "I don't blame her. My efficient and conscientious chargé d'affaires, Mr. Thrombley, felt that I should reach the Embassy, here, as soon as possible, and from where she was standing, it must have looked like a kidnapping. Fact is, it looked like one from where I was standing, too. Was that you and your people who were chasing us? Then I must apologize for opening fire on you...I hope nobody was hurt."

"No, our cars are pretty well armored. You scored a couple of times on one of them, but no harm done. I reckon after what happened to Silas Cumshaw, you had a right to be suspicious."

I noticed that refreshments, including several bottles, had been placed on a big wicker table under the arched veranda.

"Can I offer you a drink, Captain, in token of mutual amity?" I asked.

"Well, now, I'd like to, Mr. Ambassador, but I'm on duty…" he began.

"You can't be. You're an officer of the Planetary Government of New Texas, and in this Embassy, you're in the territory of the Solar League."

"That's right, now, Mr. Ambassador," he grinned. "Extraterritoriality. Wonderful thing, extraterritoriality." He looked at Hoddy, who, for the first time since I had met him, was trying to shrink into the background. "And diplomatic immunity, too. Ain't it, Hoddy?"

After he had had his drink and departed, we all sat down. Thrombley began speaking almost at once.

"Mr. Ambassador, you must, you simply must, issue a public statement, immediately, sir. Only a public statement, issued promptly, will relieve the crisis into which we have all been thrust."

"Oh, come, Mr. Thrombley," I objected. "Captain Nelson'll take care of all that in his report to his superiors."

Thrombley looked at me for a moment as though I had been speaking to him in Hottentot, then waved his hands in polite exasperation.

"Oh, no, no! I don't mean that, sir. I mean a public statement to the effect that you have assumed full responsibility for the Embassy. Where is that thing? Mr. Gomez!"

Gomez gave him four or five sheets, stapled together. He laid them on the table, turned to the last sheet, and whipped out a pen.

"Here, sir; just sign here."

"Are you crazy?" I demanded. "I'll be damned if I'll sign that. Not till I've taken an inventory of the physical property of the Embassy, and familiarized myself with all its commitments, and had the books audited by some firm of certified public accountants."

Thrombley and Gomez looked at one another. They both groaned.

"But we must have a statement of assumption of responsibility..." Gomez dithered.

"...or the business of the Embassy will be at a dead stop, and we can't do anything," Thrombley finished.

"Wait a moment, Thrombley," Stonehenge cut in. "I understand Mr. Silk's attitude. I've taken command of a good many ships and installations, at one time or another, and I've never signed for anything I couldn't see and feel and count. I know men who retired as brigadier generals or vice-admirals, but they retired loaded with debts incurred because as second lieutenants or ensigns they forgot that simple rule."

He turned to me. "Without any disrespect to the chargé d'affaires, Mr. Silk, this Embassy has been pretty badly disorganized since Mr. Cumshaw's death. No one felt authorized, or, to put it more accurately, no one dared, to declare himself acting head of the Embassy—"

"Because that would make him the next target?" I interrupted. "Well, that's what I was sent here for. Mr. Gomez, as Secretary of the Embassy, will you please, at once, prepare a statement for the press and telecast release to the effect that I am now the authorized head of this Embassy, responsible from this hour for all its future policies and all its present commitments insofar as they obligate the government of the Solar League. Get that out at once. Tomorrow, I will present my credentials to the Secretary of State here. Thereafter, Mr. Thrombley, you can rest in the assurance that I'll be the one they'll be shooting at."

"But you can't wait that long, Mr. Ambassador," Thrombley almost wailed. "We must go immediately to the Statehouse. The reception for you is already going on."

I looked at my watch, which had been regulated aboard ship for Capella IV time. It was just 1315.

"What time do they hold diplomatic receptions on this planet, Mr. Thrombley?" I asked.

"Oh, any time at all, sir. This one started about 0900 when the news that the ship was in orbit off-planet got in. It'll be a barbecue, of course, and—"

"Barbecued supercow! Yipeee!" Hoddy yelled. "What I been waitin' for for five years!"

It would be the vilest cruelty not to take him along, I thought. And it would also keep him and Stonehenge apart for a while.

"But we must hurry, Mr. Ambassador," Thrombley was saying. "If you will change, now, to formal dress..."

And he was looking at me, gasping. I think it was the first time he had actually seen what I was wearing.

"In native dress, Mr. Ambassador!"

Thrombley's eyes and tone were again those of an innocent spaniel caught in the middle of a marital argument.

Then his gaze fell to my belt and his eyes became saucers. "Oh, dear! And armed!"

My chargé d'affaires was shuddering and he could not look directly at me.

"Mr. Ambassador, I understand that you were recently appointed from the Consular Service. I sincerely hope that you will not take it amiss if I point out, here in private, that—"

"Mr. Thrombley, I am wearing this costume and these pistols on the direct order of Secretary of State Ghopal Singh."

That set him back on his heels.

"I...I can't believe it!" he exclaimed. "An ambassador is *never* armed."

"Not when he's dealing with a government which respects the comity of nations and the usages of diplomatic practice, no," I replied. "But the fate of Mr. Cumshaw clearly indicates that the government of New Texas is not such a government. These pistols are in the nature of a not-too-subtle hint of the manner in which this government, here, is being regarded by the government of the Solar League." I turned to Stonehenge. "Commander, what sort of an Embassy guard have we?" I asked.

"Space Marines, sergeant and five men. I double as guard officer, sir."

"Very well. Mr. Thrombley insists that it is necessary for me to go to this fish-fry or whatever it is immediately. I want two men, a driver and an auto-rifleman, for my car. And from now on, I would suggest, Commander, that you wear your sidearm at all times outside the Embassy."

"Yes, sir!" and this time, Stonehenge gave me a real salute.

"Well, I must phone the Statehouse, then," Thrombley said. "We will have to call on Secretary of State Palme, and then on President Hutchinson."

With that, he got up, excused himself, motioned Gomez to follow, and hurried away.

I got up, too, and motioned Stonehenge aside.

"Aboard ship, coming in, I was told that there's a task force of the Space Navy on maneuvers about five light-years from here," I said.

"Yes, sir. Task Force Red-Blue-Green, Fifth Space Fleet. Fleet Admiral Sir Rodney Tregaskis."

"Can we get hold of a fast space-boat, with hyperdrive engines, in a hurry?"

"Eight or ten of them always around New Austin spaceport, available for charter."

"All right; charter one and get out to that fleet. Tell Admiral Tregaskis that the Ambassador at New Austin feels in need of protection; possibility of z'Srauff invasion. I'll give you written orders. I want the Fleet within radio call. How far out would that be, with our facilities?"

"The Embassy radio isn't reliable beyond about sixty light-minutes, sir."

"Then tell Sir Rodney to bring his fleet in that close. The invasion, if it comes, will probably not come from the direction of the z'Srauff star-cluster; they'll probably jump past us and move in from the other side. I hope you don't think I'm having nightmares, Commander. Danger of a z'Srauff invasion was pointed out to me by persons on the very highest level, on Luna."

Stonehenge nodded. "I'm always having the same kind of nightmares, sir. Especially since this special envoy arrived here, ostensibly to negotiate a meteor-mining treaty." He hesitated for a moment. "We don't want the New Texans to know, of course, that you've sent for the fleet?"

"Naturally not."

"Well, if I can wait till about midnight before I leave, I can get a boat owned, manned and operated by Solar League people. The boat's a dreadful-looking old tub, but she's sound and fast. The gang who own her are pretty notorious characters—suspected of smuggling, piracy, and what not—but they'll keep their mouths shut if well paid."

"Then pay them well," I said. "And it's just as well you're not leaving at once. When I get back from this clambake, I'll want to have a general informal council, and I certainly want you in on it."

On the way to the Statehouse in the aircar, I kept wondering just how smart I had been.

I was pretty sure that the z'Srauff was getting ready for a sneak attack on New Texas, and, as Solar League Ambassador, I of course had the right to call on the Space Navy for any amount of armed protection.

Sending Stonehenge off on what couldn't be less than an eighteen-hour trip would delay anything he and Hoddy might be cooking up, too.

On the other hand, with the fleet so near, they might decide to have me rubbed out in a hurry, to justify seizing the planet ahead of the z'Srauff.

I was in that pleasant spot called, "Damned if you do and damned if you don't…"

CHAPTER FOUR

The Statehouse appeared to cover about a square mile of ground and it was an insane jumble of buildings piled beside and on top of one another, as though it had been in continuous construction ever since the planet was colonized, eighty-odd years before.

At what looked like one of the main entrances, the car stopped. I told our Marine driver and auto-rifleman to park the car and take in the barbecue, but to leave word with the doorman where they could be found. Hoddy, Thrombley and I then went in, to be met by a couple of New Texas Rangers, one of them the officer who had called at the Embassy. They guided us to the office of the Secretary of State.

"We're dreadfully late," Thrombley was fretting. "I do hope we haven't kept the Secretary waiting too long."

From the looks of him, I was afraid we had. He jumped up from his desk and hurried across the room as soon as the receptionist opened the door for us, his hand extended.

"Good afternoon, Mr. Thrombley," he burbled nervously. "And this is the new Ambassador, I suppose. And this—" He caught sight of Hoddy Ringo, bringing up the rear and stopped short, hand flying to open mouth. "Oh, dear me!"

So far, I had been building myself a New Texas stereotype from Hoddy Ringo and the Ranger officer who had chased us to the Embassy. But this frightened little rabbit of a fellow simply didn't fit it. An alien would be justified in assigning him to an entirely different species.

Thrombley introduced me. I introduced Hoddy as my confidential secretary and advisor. We all shook hands, and Thrombley dug my credentials out of his briefcase and handed them to me, and I handed them to the Secretary of State, Mr. William A. Palme. He barely glanced at them, then shook my hand again fervently and mumbled something about "inexpressible pleasure" and "entirely acceptable to my government."

That made me the accredited and accepted Ambassador to New Texas.

Mr. Palme hoped, or said he hoped, that my stay in New Texas would be long and pleasant. He seemed rather less than convinced that it would be. His eyes kept returning in horrified fascination to my belt. Each time they would focus on the butts of my Krupp-Tattas, he would pull them resolutely away again.

"And now, we must take you to President Hutchinson; he is most anxious to meet you, Mr. Silk. If you will please come with me..."

Four or five Rangers who had been loitering the hall outside moved to follow us as we went toward the elevator. Although we had come into the building onto a floor only a few feet above street-level, we went down three floors from the hallway outside the Secretary of State's office, into a huge room, the concrete floor of which was oil-stained, as though vehicles were continually being driven in and out. It was about a hundred feet wide, and two or three hundred in length. Daylight was visible through open doors at the end. As we approached them, the Rangers fanning out on either side and in front of us, I could hear a perfect bedlam of noise outside—shouting, singing, dance-band music, interspersed with the banging of shots.

When we reached the doors at the end, we emerged into one end of a big rectangular plaza, at least five hundred yards in length. Most of the uproar was centered at the opposite end, where several thousand people, in costumes colored through the whole spectrum, were milling about. There seemed to be at least two square-dances going on, to the music of competing bands. At the distant end of the plaza, over the heads of the crowd, I could see the piles and tracks of an overhead crane, towering above what looked like an open-hearth furnace. Between us and the bulk of the crowd, in a cleared space, two medium tanks, heavily padded with mats, were ramming and trying to overturn each other, the mob of spectators crowding as close to them as they dared. The din was positively deafening, though we were at least two hundred yards from the center of the crowd.

"Oh, dear, I always dread these things!" Palme was saying.

"Yes, absolutely anything could happen," Thrombley twittered.

"Man, this is a real barbecue!" Hoddy gloated. "Now I really feel at home!"

"Over this way, Mr. Silk," Palme said, guiding me toward the short end of the plaza, on our left. "We will see the President and then…"

He gulped.

"…then we will all go to the barbecue."

In the center of the short end of the plaza, dwarfed by the monster bulks of steel and concrete and glass around it, stood a little old building of warm-tinted adobe. I had never seen it before, but somehow it was familiar-looking.

And then I remembered. Although I had never seen it before, I had seen it pictured many times; pictured under attack, with gunsmoke spouting from windows and parapets.

I plucked Thrombley's sleeve.

"Isn't that a replica of the Alamo?"

He was shocked. "Oh, dear, Mr. Ambassador, don't let anybody hear you ask that. That's no replica. It *is* the Alamo. *The* Alamo."

I stood there a moment, looking at it. I was remembering, and finally understanding, what my psycho-history lessons about the "Romantic Freeze" had meant.

They had taken this little mission-fort down, brick by adobe brick, loaded it carefully into a spaceship, brought it here, forty two light-years away from Terra, and reverently set it up again. Then they had built a whole world and a whole social philosophy around it.

It had been the dissatisfied, of course, the discontented, the dreamers, who had led the vanguard of man's explosion into space following the discovery of the hyperspace-drive. They had gone from Terra cherishing dreams of things that had been dumped into the dust bin of history, carrying with them pictures of ways of life that had passed away, or that had never really been. Then, in their new life, on new planets, they had set to work making those dreams and those pictures live.

And, many times, they had come close to succeeding.

These Texans, now: they had left behind the cold fact that it had been their state's great industrial complex that had made their migration possible. They ignored the fact that their life here on Capella IV was possible only by application of modern industrial technology. That rodeo down the plaza—tank-tilting instead of bronco-busting.

Here they were, living frozen in a romantic dream, a world of roving cowboys and ranch kingdoms.

No wonder Hoddy hadn't liked the books I had been reading on the ship. They shook the fabric of that dream.

There were people moving about, at this relatively quiet end of the plaza, mostly in the direction of the barbecue. Ten or twelve Rangers loitered at the front of the Alamo, and with them I saw the dress blues of my two Marines. There was a little three-wheeled motorcart among them, from which they were helping themselves to food and drink. When they saw us coming, the two Marines shoved their sandwiches into the hands of a couple of Rangers and tried to come to attention.

"At ease, at ease," I told them. "Have a good time, boys. Hoddy, you better get in on some of this grub; I may be inside for quite a while."

As soon as the Rangers saw Hoddy, they hastily got things out of their right hands. Hoddy grinned at them.

"Take it easy, boys," he said. "I'm protected by the game laws. I'm a diplomat, I am."

There were a couple of Rangers lounging outside the door of the President's office and both of them carried autorifles, implying things I didn't like.

I had seen the President of the Solar League wandering around the dome-city of Artemis unattended, looking for all the world like a professor in his academic halls. Since then, maybe before then, I had always had a healthy suspicion of governments whose chiefs had to surround themselves with bodyguards.

But the President of New Texas, John Hutchinson, was alone in his office when we were shown in. He got up and came around his desk to greet us, a slender, stoop-shouldered man in a black-and-gold laced jacket. He had a narrow compressed mouth and eyes that seemed to be watching every corner of the room at once. He wore a pair of small pistols in cross-body holsters under his coat, and he always kept one hand or the other close to his abdomen.

He was like, and yet unlike, the Secretary of State. Both had the look of hunted animals; but where Palme was a rabbit, twitching to take flight at the first whiff of danger, Hutchinson was a cat who hears hounds baying—ready to run if he could, or claw if he must.

"Good day, Mr. Silk," he said, shaking hands with me after the introductions. "I see you're heeled; you're smart. You wouldn't be here today if poor Silas Cumshaw'd been as smart as you are. Great man, though; a wise and farseeing statesman. He and I were real friends."

"You know who Mr. Silk brought with him as bodyguard?" Palme asked. "Hoddy Ringo!"

"Oh, my God! I thought this planet was rid of him!" The President turned to me. "You got a good trigger-man, though, Mr. Ambassador. Good man to watch your back for you. But lot of folks here won't thank you for bringing him back to New Texas."

He looked at his watch. "We have time for a little drink, before we go outside, Mr. Silk," he said. "Care to join me?"

I assented and he got a bottle of superbourbon out of his desk, with four glasses. Palme got some water tumblers and brought the pitcher of ice-water from the cooler.

I noticed that the New Texas Secretary of State filled his three-ounce liquor glass to the top and gulped it down at once. He might act as though he were descended from a long line of maiden aunts, but he took his liquor in blasts that would have floored a spaceport labor-boss.

We had another drink, a little slower, and chatted for a while, and then Hutchinson said, regretfully that we'd have to go outside and meet the folks. Outside, our guards—Hoddy, the two Marines, the Rangers who had escorted us from Palme's office, and Hutchinson's retinue—surrounded us, and we made our way down the plaza, through the crowd. The din—ear-piercing yells, whistles, cowbells, pistol shots, the cacophony of the two dance-bands, and the chorus-singing, of which I caught only the words: *The skies of freedom are above you!*—was as bad as New Year's Eve in Manhattan or Nairobi or New Moscow, on Terra.

"Don't take all this as a personal tribute, Mr. Silk!" Hutchinson screamed into my ear. "On this planet, to paraphrase Nietzsche, a good barbecue halloweth any cause!"

That surprised me, at the moment. Later I found out that John Hutchinson was one of the leading scholars on New Texas and had once been president of one of their universities. New Texas Christian, I believe.

As we got up onto the platform, close enough to the barbecue pits to feel the heat from them, somebody let off what sounded like a fifty-mm anti-tank gun five or six times. Hutchinson grabbed a microphone and bellowed into it: "Ladies and gentlemen! Your attention, please!"

The noise began to diminish, slowly, until I could hear one voice, in the crowd below:

"Shut up, you damn fools! We can't eat till this is over!"

Hutchinson introduced me, in very few words. I gathered that lengthy speeches at barbecues were not popular on New Texas.

"Ladies and gentlemen!" I yelled into the microphone. "Appreciative as I am of this honor, there is one here who is more deserving of your notice than I; one to whom I, also, pay homage. He's over there on the fire, and I want a slice of him as soon as possible!"

That got a big ovation. There was, beside the water pitcher, a bottle of superbourbon. I ostentatiously threw the water out of the glass, poured a big shot of the corrosive stuff, and downed it.

"For God's sake, let's eat!" I finished. Then I turned to Thrombley, who was looking like a priest who has just seen the bishop spit in the holy-water font. "Stick close to me," I whispered. "Cue me in on the local notables, and the other members of the Diplomatic Corps." Then we all got down off the platform, and a band climbed up and began playing one of those raucous "cowboy ballads" which had originated in Manhattan about the middle of the Twentieth Century.

"The sandwiches'll be here in a moment, Mr. Ambassador," Hutchinson screamed—in effect, whispered—in my ear. "Don't feel any reluctance about shaking hands with a sandwich in your other hand; that's standard practice, here. You struck just the right note, up there. That business with the liquor was positively inspired!"

The sandwiches—huge masses of meat and hot relish, wrapped in tortillas of some sort—arrived and I bit into one.

I'd been eating supercow all my life, frozen or electron-beamed for transportation, and now I was discovering that I had never really eaten supercow before. I finished the first sandwich in surprisingly short order and was starting on my second when the crowd began coming.

First, the Diplomatic Corps, the usual collection of weirdies, human and otherwise...

There was the Ambassador from Tara, in a suit of what his planet produced as a substitute for Irish homespuns. His Embassy, if it was like the others I had seen elsewhere, would be an outsize cottage with whitewashed walls and a thatched roof, with a bowl of milk outside the door for the Little People…

The Ambassador from Alpheratz II, the South African Nationalist planet, with a full beard, and old fashioned plug hat and tail-coat. They were a frustrated lot. They had gone into space to practice *apartheid* and had settled on a planet where there was no other intelligent race to be superior to…

The Mormon Ambassador from Deseret—Delta Camelopardalis V…

The Ambassador from Spica VII, a short jolly-looking little fellow, with a head like a seal's, long arms, short legs and a tail like a kangaroo's…

The Ambassador from Beta Cephus VI, who could have passed for human if he hadn't had blood with a copper base instead of iron. His skin was a dark green and his hair was a bright blue…

I was beginning to correct my first impression that Thrombley was a complete dithering fool. He stood at my left elbow, whispering the names and governments and home planets of the Ambassadors as they came up, handing me little slips of paper on which he had written phonetically correct renditions of the greetings I would give them in their own language. I was still twittering a reply to the greeting of Nanadabadian, from Beta Cephus VI, when he whispered to me:

"Here it comes, sir. The z'Srauff!"

The z'Srauff were reasonably close to human stature and appearance, allowing for the fact that their ancestry had been canine instead of simian. They had, of course, longer and narrower jaws than we have, and definitely carnivorous teeth.

There were stories floating around that they enjoyed barbecued Terran even better than they did supercow and hot relish.

This one advanced, extending his three-fingered hand.

"I am most happy to make connection with Solar League representative," he said. "I am named Gglafrr Ddespttann Vuvuvu."

No wonder Thrombley let him introduce himself. I answered in the Basic English that was all he'd admit to understanding:

"The name of your great nation has gone before you to me. The stories we tell to our young of you are at the top of our books. I have hope to make great pleasure in you and me to be friends."

Gglafrr Vuvuvu's smile wavered a little at the oblique reference to the couple of trouncings our Space Navy had administered to z'Srauff ships in the past. "We will be in the same place again times with no number," the alien replied. "I have hope for you that time you are in this place will be long and will put pleasure in your heart."

Then the pressure of the line behind him pushed him on. Cabinet Members; Senators and Representatives; prominent citizens, mostly Judge so-and-so, or Colonel this-or-that. It was all a blur, so much so that it was an instant before I recognized the gleaming golden hair and the statuesque figure.

"Thank you! I have met the Ambassador." The lovely voice was shaking with restrained anger.

"Gail!" I exclaimed.

"Your father coming to the barbecue, Gail?" President Hutchinson was asking.

"He ought to be here any minute. He sent me on ahead from the hotel. He wants to meet the Ambassador. That's why I joined the line."

"Well, suppose I leave Mr. Silk in your hands for a while," Hutchinson said. "I ought to circulate around a little."

"Yes. Just leave him in my hands!" she said vindictively.

"What's wrong, Gail?" I wanted to know. "I know, I was supposed to meet you at the spaceport, but—"

"You made a beautiful fool of me at the spaceport!"

"Look, I can explain everything. My Embassy staff insisted on hurrying me off—"

Somebody gave a high-pitched whoop directly behind me and emptied the clip of a pistol. I couldn't even hear what else I said. I couldn't hear what she said, either, but it was something angry.

"You have to listen to me!" I roared in her ear. "I can explain everything!"

"Any diplomat can explain anything!" she shouted back.

"Look, Gail, you're hanging an innocent man!" I yelled back at her. "I'm entitled to a fair trial!"

Somebody on the platform began firing his pistol within inches of the loud-speakers and it sounded like an H-bomb going off. She grabbed my wrist and dragged me toward a door under the platform.

"Down here!" she yelled. "And this better be good, Mr. Silk!"

We went down a spiral ramp, lighted by widely-scattered overhead lights.

"Space-attack shelter," she explained. "And look: what goes on in space-ships is one thing, but it's as much as a girl's reputation is worth to come down here during a barbecue."

There seemed to be quite few girls at that barbecue who didn't care what happened to their reputations. We discovered that after looking into a couple of passageways that branched off the entrance.

"Over this way," Gail said, "Confederate Courts Building. There won't be anything going on over here, now."

I told her, with as much humorous detail as possible, about how Thrombley had shanghaied me to the Embassy, and about the chase by the Rangers. Before I was half through, she was laughing heartily, all traces of her anger gone. Finally, we came to a stairway, and at the head of it to a small door.

"It's been four years that I've been away from here," she said. "I think there's a reading room of the Law Library up here. Let's go in and enjoy the quiet for a while."

But when we opened the door, there was a Ranger standing inside.

"Come to see a trial, Mr. Silk? Oh, hello, Gail. Just in time; they're going to prepare for the next trial."

As he spoke, something clicked at the door. Gail looked at me in consternation.

"Now we're locked in," she said. "We can't get out till the trial's over."

CHAPTER FIVE

I looked around.

We were on a high balcony, at the end of a long, narrow room. In front of us, windows rose to the ceiling, and it was evident that the floor of the room was about twenty feet below ground level. Outside, I could see the barbecue still going on, but not a murmur of noise penetrated to us. What seemed to be the judge's bench was against the outside wall, under the tall windows. To the right of it was a railed stand with a chair in it, and in front, arranged in U-shape, were three tables at which a number of men were hastily conferring. There were nine judges in a row on the bench, all in black gowns. The spectators' seats below were filled with people, and there were quite a few up here on the balcony.

"What is this? Supreme Court?" I asked as Gail piloted me to a couple of seats where we could be alone.

"No, Court of Political Justice," she told me. "This is the court that's going to try those three Bonney brothers, who killed Mr. Cumshaw."

It suddenly occurred to me that this was the first time I had heard anything specific about the death of my predecessor.

"That isn't the trial that's going on now, I hope?"

"Oh, no; that won't be for a couple of days. Not till after you can arrange to attend. I don't know what this trial is. I only got home today, myself."

"What's the procedure here?" I wanted to know.

"Well, those nine men are judges," she began. "The one in the middle is President Judge Nelson. You've met his son—the Ranger officer who chased you from the spaceport. He's a regular jurist. The other eight are prominent citizens who are drawn from a panel, like a jury. The men at the table on the left are the prosecution: friends of the politician who was killed. And the ones on the right are the defense: they'll try to prove that the dead man got what was coming to him. The ones in the middle are friends of the court: they're just anybody who has any interest in the case—people who want to get some point of law cleared up, or see some precedent established, or something like that."

"You seem to assume that this is a homicide case," I mentioned.

"They generally are. Sometimes mayhem, or wounding, or simple assault, but—"

There had been some sort of conference going on in the open space of floor between the judges' bench and the three tables. It broke up, now, and the judge in the middle rapped with his gavel.

"Are you gentlemen ready?" he asked. "All right, then. Court of Political Justice of the Confederate Continents of New Texas is now in session. Case of the friends of S. Austin Maverick, deceased, late of James Bowie Continent, versus Wilbur Whately."

"My God, did somebody finally kill Aus Maverick?" Gail whispered.

On the center table, in front of the friends of the court, both sides seemed to have piled their exhibits; among the litter I saw some torn clothing, a big white sombrero covered with blood, and a long machete.

"The general nature of the case," the judge was saying, "is that the defendant, Wilbur Whately, of Sam Houston Continent, is here charged with divers offenses arising from the death of the Honorable S. Austin Maverick, whom he killed on the front steps of the Legislative Assembly Building, here in New Austin…"

What goes on here? I thought angrily. *This is the rankest instance of a pre-judged case I've ever seen.* I started to say as much to Gail, but she hushed me.

"I want to hear the specifications," she said.

A man at the prosecution table had risen.

"Please the court," he began, "the defendant, Wilbur Whately, is here charged with political irresponsibility and excessive atrocity in exercising his constitutional right of criticism of a practicing politician.

"The specifications are, as follows: That, on the afternoon of May Seventh, Anno Domini 2193, the defendant here present did arm himself with a machete, said machete not being one of his normal and accustomed weapons, and did loiter in wait on the front steps of the Legislative Assembly Building in the city of New Austin, Continent of Sam Houston, and did approach the decedent, addressing him in abusive, obscene, and indecent language, and did set upon and attack him with the machete aforesaid, causing the said decedent, S. Austin Maverick, to die."

The court wanted to know how the defendant would plead. Somebody, without bothering to rise, said, "Not guilty, Your Honor," from the defense table.

There was a brief scraping of chairs; four of five men from the defense and the prosecution tables got up and advanced to confer in front of the bench, comparing sheets of paper. The man who had read the charges, obviously the chief prosecutor, made himself the spokesman.

"Your Honor, defense and prosecution wish to enter the following stipulations: That the decedent was a practicing politician within the meaning of the Constitution, that he met his death in the manner stated in the coroner's report, and that he was killed by the defendant, Wilbur Whately."

"Is that agreeable to you, Mr. Vincent?" the judge wanted to know.

The defense answered affirmatively. I sat back, gaping like a fool. Why, that was practically—no, it *was*—a confession.

"All right, gentlemen," the judge said. "Now we have all that out of the way, let's get on with the case."

As though there were any case to get on with! I fully expected them to take it on from there in song, words by Gilbert and music by Sullivan.

"Well, Your Honor, we have a number of character witnesses," the prosecution—prosecution, for God's sake!—announced.

"Skip them," the defense said. "We stipulate."

"But you can't stipulate character testimony," the prosecution argued. "You don't know what our witnesses are going to testify to."

"Sure we do: they're going to give us a big long shaggy-dog story about the Life and Miracles of Saint Austin Maverick. We'll agree in advance to all that; this case is concerned only with his record as a politician. And as he spent the last fifteen years in the Senate, that's all a matter of public record. I assume that the prosecution is going to introduce all that, too?"

"Well, naturally..." the prosecutor began.

"Including his public acts on the last day of his life?" the counsel for the defense demanded. "His actions on the morning of May seventh as chairman of the Finance and Revenue Committee? You going to introduce that as evidence for the prosecution?"

"Well, now…" the prosecutor began.

"Your Honor, we ask to have a certified copy of the proceedings of the Senate Finance and Revenue Committee for the morning of May Seventh, 2193, read into the record of this court," the counsel for the defense said. "And thereafter, we rest our case."

"Has the prosecution anything to say before we close the court?" Judge Nelson inquired.

"Well, Your Honor, this seems…that is, we ought to hear both sides of it. My old friend, Aus Maverick, was really a fine man; he did a lot of good for the people of his continent…"

"Yeah, we'd of lynched him, when he got back, if somebody hadn't chopped him up here in New Austin!" a voice from the rear of the courtroom broke in.

The prosecution hemmed and hawed for a moment, and then announced, in a hasty mumble, that it rested.

"I will now close the court," Judge Nelson said. "I advise everybody to keep your seats. I don't think it's going to be closed very long."

And then, he actually closed the court; pressing a button on the bench, he raised a high black screen in front of him and his colleagues. It stayed up for some sixty seconds, and then dropped again.

"The Court of Political Justice has reached a verdict," he announced. "Wilbur Whately, and your attorney, approach and hear the verdict."

The defense lawyer motioned a young man who had been sitting beside him to rise. In the silence that had fallen, I could hear the defendant's boots squeaking as he went forward to hear his fate. The judge picked up a belt and a pair of pistols that had been lying in front of him.

"Wilbur Whately," he began, "this court is proud to announce that you have been unanimously acquitted of the charge of political irresponsibility, and of unjustified and excessive atrocity.

"There was one dissenting vote on acquitting you of the charge of political irresponsibility; one of the associate judges felt that the late unmitigated scoundrel, Austin Maverick, ought to have been skinned alive, an inch at a time. You are, however, acquitted of that charge, too.

"You all know," he continued, addressing the entire assemblage, "the reason for which this young hero cut down that monster of political iniquity, S. Austin Maverick. On the very morning of his justly-merited death, Austin Maverick, using the powers of his political influence, rammed through the Finance and Revenue Committee a bill entitled 'An Act for the Taxing of Personal Incomes, and for the Levying of a Withholding Tax.' Fellow citizens, words fail me to express my horror of this diabolic proposition, this proposed instrument of tyrannical extortion, borrowed from the Dark Ages of the Twentieth Century! Why, if this young nobleman had not taken his blade in hand, I'd have killed the sonofabitch, myself!"

He leaned forward, extending the belt and holsters to the defendant.

"I therefore restore to you your weapons, taken from you when, in compliance with the law, you were formally arrested. Buckle them on, and, assuming your weapons again, go forth from this court a free man, Wilbur Whately.

And take with you that machete with which you vindicated the liberties and rights of all New Texans. Bear it reverently to your home, hang it among your lares and penates, cherish it, and dying, mention it within your will, bequeathing it as a rich legacy unto your issue! Court adjourned; next session 0900 tomorrow. For Chrissake, let's get out of here before the barbecue's over!"

Some of the spectators, drooling for barbecued supercow, began crowding and jostling toward the exits; more of them were pushing to the front of the courtroom, cheering and waving their hip-flasks. The prosecution and about half of the friends of the court hastily left by a side door, probably to issue statements disassociating themselves from the deceased Maverick.

"So that's the court that's going to try the men who killed Ambassador Cumshaw," I commented, as Gail and I went out. "Why, the purpose of that court seems to be to acquit murderers."

"Murderers?" She was indignant. "That wasn't murder. He just killed a politician. All the court could do was determine whether or not the politician needed it, and while I never heard about Maverick's income-tax proposition, I can't see how they could have brought in any other kind of a verdict. Of all the outrageous things!"

I WAS thoughtfully silent as we went out into the plaza, which was still a riot of noise and polychromatic costumes. And my thoughts were as weltered as the scene before me.

Apparently, on New Texas, killing a politician wasn't regarded as *mallum in se*, and was *mallum prohibitorum* only to the extent that what happened to the politician was in excess of what he deserved. I began to understand why Palme was such a scared rabbit, why Hutchinson had that hunted look and kept his hands always within inches of his pistols.

I began to feel more pity than contempt for Thrombley, too. *He's been on this planet too long and he should never have been sent here in the first place. I'll rotate him home as soon as possible...*

Then the full meaning of what I had seen finally got through to me: if they were going to try the killers of Cumshaw in that court, that meant that on New Texas, foreign diplomats were regarded as practicing politicians...

That made me a practicing politician too!

And that's why, when we got back to the vicinity of the bandstand, I had my right hand close to my pistol, with my thumb on the inconspicuous little spot of silver inlay that operated the secret holster mechanism.

I saw Hutchinson and Palme and Thrombley ahead. With them was a newcomer, a portly, ruddy-faced gentleman with a white mustache and goatee, dressed in a white suit. Gail broke away from me and ran toward him. This, I thought, would be her father; now I would be introduced and find out just what her last name was. I followed, more slowly, and saw a waiter, with a wheeled serving-table, move in behind the group which she had joined.

So I saw what none of them did—the waiter suddenly reversed his long carving-knife and poised himself for a blow at President Hutchinson's back. I simply pressed the little silver stud on my belt, the Krupp-Tatta popped obediently out of the holster into my open hand. I thumbed off the safety and swung up; when my sights closed on the rising hand that held the knife, I fired.

Hoddy Ringo, who had been holding a sandwich with one hand and a drink with the other, dropped both and jumped on the man whose hand I had smashed. A couple of Rangers closed in and grabbed him, also. The group around President Hutchinson had all turned and were staring from me to the man I had shot, and from him to the knife with the broken handle, lying on the ground.

Hutchinson spoke first. "Well, Mr. Ambassador! My Government thanks your Government! That was nice shooting!"

"Hey, you been holdin' out on me!" Hoddy accused. "I never knew you was that kinda gunfighter!"

"There's a new wrinkle," the man with the white goatee said. "We'll have to screen the help at these affairs a little more closely." He turned to me. "Mr. Ambassador, New Texas owes you a great deal for saving the President's life. If you'll get that pistol out of your hand, I'd be proud to shake it, sir."

I holstered my automatic, and took his hand. Gail was saying, "Stephen, this is my father," and at the same time, Palme, the Secretary of State, was doing it more formally:

"Ambassador Silk, may I present one of our leading citizens and large ranchers, Colonel Andrew Jackson Hickock."

Dumbarton Oaks had taught me how to maintain the proper diplomat's unchanging expression; drinking superbourbon had been a post-graduate course. I needed that training as I finally learned Gail's last name.

It was early evening before we finally managed to get away from the barbecue. Thrombley had called the Embassy and told them not to wait dinner for us, so the staff had finished eating and were relaxing in the patio when our car came in through the street gate. Stonehenge and another man came over to meet us as we got out—a man I hadn't met before.

He was a little fellow, half-Latin, half-Oriental; in New Texas costume and wearing a pair of pistols like mine, in State Department Special Services holsters. He didn't look like a Dumbarton Oaks product: I thought he was more likely an alumnus of some private detective agency.

"Mr. Francisco Parros, our Intelligence man," Stonehenge introduced him.

"Sorry I wasn't here when you arrived, Mr. Silk," Parros said. "Out checking on some things. But I saw that bit of shooting, on the telecast screen in a bar over town. You know, there was a camera right over the bandstand that caught the whole thing—you and Miss Hickock coming toward the President and his party, Miss Hickock running forward to her father, the waiter going up behind Hutchinson with the knife, and then that beautiful draw and snap shot. They ran it again a couple of times on the half-hourly newscast. Everybody in New Austin, maybe on New Texas, is talking about it, now."

"Yes, indeed, sir," Gomez, the Embassy Secretary, said, joining us. "You've made yourself more popular in the eight hours since you landed than poor Mr. Cumshaw had been able to do in the ten years he spent here. But, I'm afraid, sir, you've given me a good deal of work, answering your fan-mail."

We went over and sat down at one of the big tables under the arches at the side of the patio.

"Well, that's all to the good," I said. "I'm going to need a lot of local good will, in the next few weeks. No thanks, Mr. Parros," I added, as the Intelligence man picked up a bottle and made to pour for me. "I've been practically swimming in superbourbon all afternoon. A little black coffee, if you don't mind. And now, gentlemen, if you'll all be seated, we'll see what has to be done."

"A council of war, in effect, Mr. Ambassador?" Stonehenge inquired.

"Let's call it a council to estimate the situation. But I'll have to find out from you first exactly what the situation here is."

Thrombley stirred uneasily. "But sir, I confess that I don't understand. Your briefing on Luna…"

"Was practically nonexistent. I had a total of six hours to get aboard ship, from the moment I was notified that I had been appointed to this Embassy."

"Incredible!" Thrombley murmured.

I wondered what he'd say if I told him that I thought it was deliberate.

"Naturally, I spent some time on the ship reading up on this planet, but I know practically nothing about what's been going on here in, say, the last year. And all I know about the death of Mr. Cumshaw is that he is said to have been killed by three brothers named Bonney."

"So you'll want just about everything, Mr. Silk," Thrombley said. "Really, I don't know where to begin."

"Start with why and how Mr. Cumshaw was killed. The rest, I believe, will key into that."

So they began; Thrombley, Stonehenge and Parros doing the talking. It came to this:

Ever since we had first established an Embassy on New Texas, the goal of our diplomacy on this planet had been to secure it into the Solar League. And it was a goal which seemed very little closer to realization now than it had been twenty-three years before.

"You must know, by now, what politics on this planet are like, Mr. Silk," Thrombley said.

"I have an idea. One Ambassador gone native, another gone crazy, the third killed himself, the fourth murdered."

"Yes, indeed. I've been here fifteen years, myself..."

"That's entirely too long for anybody to be stationed in this place," I told him. "If I'm not murdered, myself, in the next couple of weeks, I'm going to see that you and any other member of this staff who's been here over ten years are rotated home for a tour of duty at Department Headquarters."

"Oh, would you, Mr. Silk? I would be so happy..."

Thrombley wasn't much in the way of an ally, but at least he had a sound, selfish motive for helping me stay alive. I assured him I would get him sent back to Luna, and then went on with the discussion.

Up until six months ago, Silas Cumshaw had modeled himself after the typical New Texas politician. He had always worn at least two faces, and had always managed to place himself on every side of every issue at once. Nothing he ever said could possibly be construed as controversial. Naturally, the cause of New Texan annexation to the Solar League had made no progress whatever.

Then, one evening, at a banquet, he had executed a complete 180-degree turn, delivering a speech in which he proclaimed that union with the Solar League was the only possible way in which New Texans could retain even a vestige of local sovereignty. He had talked about an invasion as though the enemy's ships were already coming out of hyperspace, and had named the invader, calling the z'Srauff "our common enemy." The z'Srauff Ambassador, also present, had immediately gotten up and stalked out, amid a derisive chorus of barking and baying from the New Texans. The New Texans were first shocked and then wildly delighted; they had been so used to hearing nothing but inanities and high-order abstractions from their public figures that the Solar League Ambassador had become a hero overnight.

"Sounds as though there is a really strong sentiment at what used to be called the grass-roots level in favor of annexation," I commented.

"There is," Parros told me. "Of course, there is a very strong isolationist, anti-annexation, sentiment, too. The sentiment in favor of annexation is based on the point Mr. Cumshaw made—the danger of conquest by the z'Srauff. Against that, of course, there is fear of higher taxes, fear of loss of local sovereignty, fear of abrogation of local customs and institutions, and chauvinistic pride."

"We can deal with some of that by furnishing guarantees of local self-government; the emotional objections can be met by convincing them that we need the great planet of New Texas to add glory and luster to the Solar League," I said. "You think, then, that Mr. Cumshaw was assassinated by opponents of annexation?"

"Of course, sir," Thrombley replied. "These Bonneys were only hirelings. Here's what happened, on the day of the murder:

"It was the day after a holiday, a big one here on New Texas, celebrating some military victory by the Texans on Terra, a battle called San Jacinto. We didn't have any business to handle, because all the local officials were home nursing hangovers, so when Colonel Hickock called—"

"Who?" I asked sharply.

"Colonel Hickock. The father of the young lady you were so attentive to at the barbecue. He and Mr. Cumshaw had become great friends, beginning shortly before the speech the Ambassador made at that banquet. He called about 0900, inviting Mr. Cumshaw out to his ranch for the day, and as there was nothing in the way of official business, Mr. Cumshaw said he'd be out by 1030.

"When he got there, there was an aircar circling about, near the ranchhouse. As Mr. Cumshaw got out of his car and started up the front steps, somebody in this car landed it on the driveway and began shooting with a twenty-mm auto-rifle. Mr. Cumshaw was hit several times, and killed instantly."

"The fellows who did the shooting were damned lucky," Stonehenge took over. "Hickock's a big rancher. I don't know how much you know about supercow-ranching, sir, but those things have to be herded with tanks and light aircraft, so that every rancher has at his disposal a fairly good small air-armor combat team. Naturally, all the big ranchers are colonels in the Armed Reserve. Hickock has about fifteen fast fighters, and thirty medium tanks armed with fifty-mm guns. He also has some AA-guns around his ranch house—every once in a while, these ranchers get to squabbling among themselves.

"Well, these three Bonney brothers were just turning away when a burst from the ranch house caught their jet assembly, and they could only get as far as Bonneyville, thirty miles away, before they had to land. They landed right in front of the town jail.

"This Bonneyville's an awful shantytown; everybody in it is related to everybody else. The mayor, for instance, Kettle-Belly Sam Bonney, is an uncle of theirs.

"These three boys—Switchblade Joe Bonney, Jack-High Abe Bonney and Turkey-Buzzard Tom Bonney— immediately claimed sanctuary in the jail, on the grounds that they had been near to—get that; I think that indicates the line they're going to take at the trial—*near* to a political assassination. They were immediately given the protection of the jail, which is about the only well-constructed building in the place, practically a fort."

"You think that was planned in advance?" I asked.

Parros nodded emphatically. "I do. There was a hell of a big gang of these Bonneys at the jail, almost the entire able-bodied population of the place. As soon as Switchblade and Jack-High and Turkey-Buzzard landed, they were rushed inside and all the doors barred. About three minutes later, the Hickock outfit started coming in, first aircraft and then armor. They gave that town a regular Georgie Patton style blitzing."

"Yes. I'm only sorry I wasn't there to see it," Stonehenge put in. "They knocked down or burned most of the shanties, and then they went to work on the jail. The aircraft began dumping these firebombs and stun-bombs that they use to stop supercow stampedes, and the tank-guns began to punch holes in the walls. As soon as

Kettle-Belly saw what he had on his hands, he radioed a call for Ranger protection. Our friend Captain Nelson went out to see what the trouble was."

"Yes. I got the story of that from Nelson," Parros put in. "Much as he hated to do it, he had to protect the Bonneys. And as soon as he'd taken a hand, Hickock had to call off his gang. But he was smart. He grabbed everything relating to the killing—the aircar and the twenty-mm auto-rifle in particular—and he's keeping them under cover. Very few people know about that, or about the fact that on physical evidence alone, he has the killing pinned on the Bonneys so well that they'll never get away with this story of being merely innocent witnesses."

"The rest, Mr. Silk, is up to us," Thrombley said. "I have Colonel Hickock's assurance that he will give us every assistance, but we simply must see to it that those creatures with the outlandish names are convicted."

I didn't have a chance to say anything to that: at that moment, one of the servants ushered Captain Nelson toward us.

"Good evening, Captain," I greeted the Ranger. "Join us, seeing that you're on foreign soil and consequently not on duty."

He sat down with us and poured a drink.

"I thought you might be interested," he said. "We gave that waiter a going-over. We wanted to know who put him up to it. He tried to sell us the line that he was a New Texan patriot, trying to kill a tyrant, but we finally got the truth out of him. He was paid a thousand pesos to do the job, by a character they call Snake-Eyes Sam Bonney. A cousin of the three who killed Mr. Cumshaw."

"Nephew of Kettle-Belly Sam," Parros interjected. "You pick him up?"

Nelson shook his head disgustedly. "He's out in the high grass somewhere. We're still looking for him. Oh, yes, and I just heard that the trial of Switchblade, and Jack-High and Turkey-Buzzard is scheduled for three days from now. You'll be notified in due form tomorrow, but I thought you might like to know in advance."

"I certainly do, and thank you, Captain… We were just talking about you when you arrived," I mentioned. "About the arrest, or rescue, or whatever you call it, of that trio."

"Yeah. One of the jobs I'm not particularly proud of. Pity Hickock's boys didn't get hold of them before I got there. It'd of saved everybody a lot of trouble."

"Just what impression did you get at the time, Captain?" I asked. "You think Kettle-Belly knew in advance what they were going to do?"

"Sure he did. They had the whole jail fortified. Not like a jail usually is, to keep people from getting out; but like a fort, to keep people from getting in. There were no prisoners inside. I found out that they had all been released that morning."

He stopped, seemed to be weighing his words, then continued, speaking very slowly.

"Let me tell you first some things I can't testify to, couple of things that I figure went wrong with their plans.

"One of Colonel Hickock's men was on the porch to greet Mr. Cumshaw and he recognized the Bonneys. That was lucky; otherwise we might still be lookin' and wonderin' who did the shootin', which might not have been good for New Texas."

He cocked an eyebrow and I nodded. The Solar League, in similar cases, had regarded such planetary governments as due for change without notice and had promptly made the change.

"Number two," Captain Nelson continued, "that AA-shot which hit their aircar. I don't think they intended to land at the jail—it was just sort of a reserve hiding-hole. But because they'd been hit, they had to land. And they'd been slowed down so much that they couldn't dispose of the evidence before the Colonel's boys were tappin' on the door 'n' askin', couldn't they come in."

"I gather the Colonel's task-force was becoming insistent," I prompted him.

The big Ranger grinned. "Now we're on things I can testify to.

"When I got there, what had been the cell-block was on fire, and they were trying to defend the mayor's office and the warden's office. These Bonneys gave me the line that they'd been witnesses to the killing of Mr. Cumshaw by Colonel Hickock and that the Hickock outfit was trying to rub them out to keep them from testifying. I just laughed and started to walk out. Finally, they confessed that they'd shot Mr. Cumshaw, but they claimed it was right of action against political malfeasance. When they did that, I had to take them in."

"They confessed to you, before you arrested them?" I wanted to be sure of that point.

"That's right. I'm going to testify to that, Monday, when the trial is held. And that ain't all: we got their fingerprints off the car, off the gun, off some shells still in the clip, and we have the gun identified to the shells that killed Mr. Cumshaw. We got their confession fully corroborated."

I asked him if he'd give Mr. Parros a complete statement of what he'd seen and heard at Bonneyville. He was more than willing and I suggested that they go into Parros' office, where they'd be undisturbed. The Ranger and my Intelligence man got up and took a bottle of superbourbon with them. As they were leaving, Nelson turned to Hoddy, who was still with us.

"You'll have to look to your laurels, Hoddy," Nelson said. "Your Ambassador seems to be making quite a reputation for himself as a gunfighter."

"Look," Hoddy said, and though he was facing Nelson, I felt he was really talking to Stonehenge, "before I'd go up against this guy, I'd shoot myself. That way, I could be sure I'd get a nice painless job."

After they were gone, I turned to Stonehenge and Thrombley. "This seems to be a carefully prearranged killing."

They agreed.

"Then they knew *in advance* that Mr. Cumshaw would be on Colonel Hickock's front steps at about 1030. *How did they find that out?*"

"Why...why, I'm sure I don't know," Thrombley said. It was most obvious that the idea had never occurred to him before and a side glance told me that the thought was new to Stonehenge also. "Colonel Hickock called at 0900. Mr. Cumshaw left the Embassy in an aircar a few minutes later. It took an hour and a half to fly out to the Hickock ranch..."

"I don't like the implications, Mr. Silk," Stonehenge said. "I can't believe that was how it happened. In the first place, Colonel Hickock isn't that sort of man: he doesn't use his hospitality to trap people to their death. In the second place, he wouldn't have needed to use people like these Bonneys. His own men would do anything for him. In the third place, he is one of the leaders of the annexation movement here and this was obviously an anti-annexation job. And in the fourth place—"

"Hold it!" I checked him. "Are you sure he's really on the annexation side?"

He opened his mouth to answer me quickly, then closed it, waited a moment, answered me slowly. "I can guess what you are thinking, Mr. Silk. But, remember, when Colonel Hickock came here as our first Ambassador, he came here as a man with a mission. He had studied the problem and he believed in what he came for. He has never changed.

"Let me emphasize this, sir: we know he has never changed. For our own protection, we've had to check on every real leader of the annexation movement, screening them for crackpots who might do us more harm than good. The Colonel is with us all the way.

"And now, in the fourth place, underlined by what I've just said, the Colonel and Mr. Cumshaw were really friends."

"Now you're talking!" Hoddy burst in. "I've knowed A. J. ever since I was a kid. Ever since he married old Colonel MacTodd's daughter. That just ain't the way A. J. works!"

"On the other hand, Mr. Ambassador," Thrombley said, keeping his gaze fixed on Hoddy's hands and apparently ready to both duck and shut up if Hoddy moved a finger, "you will recall, I think, that Colonel Hickock did do everything in his power to see that these Bonney brothers did not reach court alive. And, let me add," he was getting bolder, tilting his chin up a little, "it's a choice as simple as this: either Colonel Hickock told them, or we have—and this is unbelievable—a traitor in the Embassy itself."

That statement rocked even Hoddy. Even though he was probably no more than one of Natalenko's little men, he still couldn't help knowing how thoroughly we were screened, indoctrinated, and—let's face it—mind-conditioned. A traitor among us was unthinkable because we just couldn't think that way.

The silence, the sorrow, were palpable. Then I remembered, told them, Hickock himself had been a Department man.

Stonehenge gripped his head between his hands and squeezed as if trying to bring out an idea. "All right, Mr. Ambassador, where are we now? Nobody who knew could have told the Bonney boys where Mr. Cumshaw would be at 1030, yet the three men were there waiting for him. You take it from there. I'm just a simple military man and I'm ready to go back to the simple military life as soon as possible."

I turned to Gomez. "There could be an obvious explanation. Bring us the official telescreen log. Let's see what calls were made. Maybe Mr. Cumshaw himself said something to someone that gave his destination away."

"That won't be necessary," Thrombley told me. "None of the junior clerks were on duty, and I took the only three calls that came in, myself. First, there was the call from Colonel Hickock. Then, the call about the wrist watch. And then, a couple of hours later, the call from the Hickock ranch, about Mr. Cumshaw's death."

"What was the call about the wrist watch?" I asked.

"Oh, that was from the z'Srauff Embassy," Thrombley said. "For some time, Mr. Cumshaw had been trying to get one of the very precise watches which the z'Srauff manufacture on their home planet. The z'Srauff Ambassador called, that day, to tell him that they had one for him and wanted to know when it was to be delivered. I told them the Ambassador was out, and they wanted to know where they could call him and I—"

I had never seen a man look more horror-stricken.

"Oh, my God! I'm the one who told them!"

What could I say? Not much, but I tried. "How could you know, Mr. Thrombley? You did the natural, the normal, the proper thing, on a call from one Ambassador to another."

I turned to the others, who, like me, preferred not to look at Thrombley. "They must have had a spy outside who told them the Ambassador had left the Embassy. Alone, right? And that was just what they'd been waiting for.

"But what's this about the watch, though. There's more to this than a simple favor from one Ambassador to another."

"My turn, Mr. Ambassador," Stonehenge interrupted. "Mr. Cumshaw had been trying to get one of the things at my insistence. Naval Intelligence is very much interested in them and we want a sample. The z'Srauff watches are very peculiar—they're operated by radium decay, which, of course is a universal constant. They're uniform to a tenth second and they're all synchronized with the official time at the capital city of the principal z'Srauff planet. The time used by the z'Srauff Navy."

Stonehenge deliberately paused, let that last phrase hang heavily in the air for a moment, then he continued.

"They're supposed to be used in religious observances—timing hours of prayer, I believe. They can, of course, have other uses.

"For example, I can imagine all those watches giving the wearer a light electric shock, or ringing a little bell, all over New Texas, at exactly the same moment. And then I can imagine all the z'Srauff running down into nice deep holes in the ground."

He looked at his own watch. "And that reminds me: my gang of pirates are at the spaceport by now, ready to blast off. I wonder if someone could drive me there."

"I'll drive him, boss," Hoddy volunteered. "I ain't doin' nothin' else."

I was wondering how I could break that up, plausibly and without betraying my suspicions, when Parros and Captain Nelson came out and joined us.

"I have a lot of stuff here," Parros said. "Stuff we never seemed to have noticed. For instance—"

I interrupted. "Commander Stonehenge's going to the spaceport, now," I said. "Suppose you ride with him, and brief him on what you learned, on the way. Then, when he's aboard, come back and tell us."

Hoddy looked at me for a long ten seconds. His expression started by being exasperated and ended by betraying grudging admiration.

CHAPTER SEVEN

The next morning, which was Saturday, I put Thrombley in charge of the routine work of the Embassy, but first instructed him to answer all inquiries about me with the statement, literally true, that I was too immersed in work of clearing up matters left unfinished after the death of the former Ambassador for any social activities. Then I called the Hickock ranch in the west end of Sam Houston Continent, mentioning an invitation the Colonel and his daughter had extended me, and told them I would be out to see them before noon that same day. With Hoddy Ringo driving the car, I arrived about 1000, and was welcomed by Gail and her father, who had flown out the evening before, after the barbecue.

Hoddy, accompanied by a Ranger and one of Hickock's ranch hands, all three disguised in shabby and grease-stained cast-offs borrowed at the ranch, and driving a dilapidated aircar from the ranch junkyard, were sent to visit the slum village of Bonneyville. They spent all day there, posing as a trio of range tramps out of favor with the law.

I spent the day with Gail, flying over the range, visiting Hickock's herd camps and slaughtering crews. It was a pleasant day and I managed to make it constructive as well.

Because of their huge size—they ran to a live weight of around fifteen tons—and their uncertain disposition, supercows are not really domesticated. Each rancher owned the herds on his own land, chiefly by virtue of constant watchfulness over them. There were always a couple of helicopters hovering over each herd, with fast fighter planes waiting on call to come in and drop fire-bombs or stun-bombs in front of them if they showed a disposition to wander too far. Naturally, things of this size could not be shipped live to the market; they were butchered on the range, and the meat hauled out in big 'copter-trucks.

Slaughtering was dangerous and exciting work. It was done with medium tanks mounting fifty-mm guns, usually working at the rear of the herd, although a supercow herd could change directions almost in a second and the killing-tanks would then find themselves in front of a stampede. I saw several such incidents. Once Gail and I had to dive in with our car and help turn such a stampede.

We got back to the ranch house shortly before dinner. Gail went at once to change clothes; Colonel Hickock and I sat down together for a drink in his library, a beautiful room. I especially admired the walls, panelled in plastic-hardened supercow-leather.

"What do you think of our planet now, Mr. Silk?" Colonel Hickock asked.

"Well, Colonel, your final message to the State was part of the briefing I received," I replied. "I must say that I agree with your opinions. Especially with your opinion of local political practices. Politics is nothing, here, if not exciting and exacting."

"You don't understand it though." That was about half-question and half-statement. "Particularly our custom of using politicians as clay pigeons."

"Well, it is rather unusual…"

"Yes." The dryness in his tone was a paragraph of comment on my understatement. "And it's fundamental to our system of government.

"You were out all afternoon with Gail; you saw how we have to handle the supercow herds. Well, it is upon the fact that every rancher must have at his disposal a powerful force of aircraft and armor, easily convertible to military uses, that our political freedom rests. You see, our government is, in effect, an oligarchy of the big landowners and ranchers, who, in combination, have enough military power to overturn any Planetary government overnight. And, on the local level, it is a paternalistic feudalism.

"That's something that would have stood the hair of any Twentieth Century 'Liberal' on end. And it gives us the freest government anywhere in the galaxy.

"There were a number of occasions, much less frequent now than formerly, when coalitions of big ranches combined their strength and marched on the Planetary government to protect their rights from government encroachment. This sort of thing could only be resorted to in defense of some inherent right, and never to infringe on the rights of others. Because, in the latter case, other armed coalitions would have arisen, as they did once or twice during the first three decades of New Texan history, to resist.

"So the right of armed intervention by the people when the government invaded or threatened their rights became an acknowledged part of our political system.

"And—this arises as a natural consequence—you can't give a man with five hundred employees and a force of tanks and aircraft the right to resist the government, then at the same time deny that right to a man who has only his own pistol or machete."

"I notice the President and the other officials have themselves surrounded by guards to protect them from individual attack," I said. "Why doesn't the government, as such, protect itself with an army and air force large enough to resist any possible coalition of the big ranchers?"

"*Because we won't let the government get that strong!*" the Colonel said forcefully. "That's one of the basic premises. We have no standing army, only the New Texas Rangers. And the legislature won't authorize any standing army, or appropriate funds to support one. Any member of the legislature who tried it would get what Austin Maverick got, a couple of weeks ago, or what Sam Saltkin got, eight years ago, when he proposed a law for the compulsory registration and licensing of firearms. The opposition to that tax scheme of Maverick's wasn't because of what it would cost the public in taxes, but from fear of what the government could do with the money after they got it.

"Keep a government poor and weak and it's your servant; let it get rich and powerful and it's your master. We don't want any masters here on New Texas."

"But the President has a bodyguard," I noted.

"Casualty rate was too high," Hickock explained. "Remember, the President's job is inherently impossible: he has to represent *all* the people."

I thought that over, could see the illogical logic, but... "How about your rancher oligarchy?"

He laughed. "Son, if I started acting like a master around this ranch in the morning, they'd find my body in an irrigation ditch before sunset.

"Sure, if you have a real army, you can keep the men under your thumb—use one regiment or one division to put down mutiny in another. But when you have only five hundred men, all of whom know everybody else and all of them armed, you just act real considerate of them if you want to keep on living."

"Then would you say that the opposition to annexation comes from the people who are afraid that if New Texas enters the Solar League, there will be League troops sent here and this…this interesting system of insuring government responsibility to the public would be brought to an end?"

"Yes. If you can show the people of this planet that the League won't interfere with local political practices, you'll have a 99.95 percent majority in favor of annexation. We're too close to the z'Srauff star-cluster, out here, not to see the benefits of joining the Solar League."

We left the Hickock ranch on Sunday afternoon and while Hoddy guided our air-car back to New Austin, I had a little time to revise some of my ideas about New Texas. That is, I had time to think during those few moments when Hoddy wasn't taking advantage of our diplomatic immunity to invent new air-ground traffic laws.

My thoughts alternated between the pleasure of remembering Gail's gay company and the gloom of understanding the complete implications of the Colonel's clarifying lectures. Against the background of his remarks, I could find myself appreciating the Ghopal-Klüng-Natalenko reasoning: the only way to cut the Gordian knot was to have another Solar League Ambassador killed.

And, whenever I could escape thinking about the fact that the next Ambassador to be the clay pigeon was me, I found myself wondering if I wanted the League to take over. Annexation, yes; New Texas customs would be protected under a treaty of annexation. But the "justified conquest" urged by Machiavelli, Jr.? No.

I was still struggling with the problem when we reached the Embassy about 1700. Everyone was there, including Stonehenge, who had returned two hours earlier with the good news that the fleet had moved into position only sixty light-minutes off Capella IV. I had reached the point in my thinking where I had decided it was useless to keep Hoddy and Stonehenge apart except as an exercise in mental agility. Inasmuch as my brain was already weight-lifting, swinging from a flying trapeze to elusive flying rings while doing triple somersaults and at the same time juggling seven Indian clubs, I skipped the whole matter.

But I'm fairly certain that it wasn't till then that Hoddy had a chance to deliver his letter-of-credence to Stonehenge.

After dinner, we gathered in my office for our coffee and a final conference before the opening of the trial the next morning.

Stonehenge spoke first, looking around the table at everyone except me.

"No matter what happens, we have the fleet within call. Sir Rodney's been active picking up those z'Srauff meteor-mining boats. They no longer have a tight screen around the system. We do. I don't think that anyone, except us, knows that the fleet's where it is."

No matter what happens, I thought glumly, and the phrase explained why he hadn't been able to look at me.

"Well, boss, I gave you my end of it, comin' in," Hoddy said. "Want me to go over it again? All right. In Bonneyville, we found half a dozen people who can swear that Kettle-Belly Sam Bonney was making preparations to protect those three brothers an hour before Ambassador Cumshaw was shot. The whole town's sorer than hell at Kettle-Belly for antagonizing the Hickock outfit and getting the place shot up the way it was. And we have witnesses that Kettle-Belly was in some kind of deal with the z'Srauff, too. The Rangers gathered up eight of them, who can swear to the preparations and to the fact that Kettle-Belly had z'Srauff visitors on different occasions before the shooting."

"That's what we want," Stonehenge said. "Something that'll connect this murder with the z'Srauff."

"Well, wait till you hear what I've got," Parros told him. "In the first place, we traced the gun and the air-car. The Bonney brothers bought them both from z'Srauff merchants, for ridiculously nominal prices. The merchant who sold the aircar is normally in the dry-goods business, and the one who sold the auto-rifle runs a toy shop. In their whole lives, those three boys never had enough money among them to pay the list price of the gun, let alone the car. That is, not until a week before the murder."

"They got prosperous, all of a sudden?" I asked.

"Yes. Two weeks before the shooting, Kettle-Belly Sam's bank account got a sudden transfusion: some anonymous benefactor deposited 250,000 pesos—about a hundred thousand dollars—to his credit. He drew out 75,000 of it and some of the money turned up again in the hands of Switchblade and Jack-High and Turkey-Buzzard. Then, a week before you landed here, he got another hundred thousand from the same anonymous source and he drew out twenty thousand of that. We think that was the money that went to pay for the attempted knife-job on Hutchinson. Two days before the barbecue, the waiter deposited a thousand at the New Austin Packers' and Shippers' Trust."

"Can you get that introduced as evidence at the trial?" I asked.

"Sure. Kettle-Belly banks at a town called Crooked Creek, about forty miles from Bonneyville. We have witnesses from the bank.

"I also got the dope on the line the Bonney brothers are going to take at the trial. They have a lawyer, Clement A. Sidney, a member of what passes for the Socialist Party on this planet. The defense will take the line of full denial of everything. The Bonneys are just three poor but honest boys who are being framed by the corrupt tools of the Big Ranching Interests."

Hoddy made an impolite noise. "Whatta we got to worry about, then?" he demanded. "They're a cinch for conviction."

"I agree with that," Stonehenge said. "If they tried to base their defense on political conviction and opposition by the Solar League, they might have a chance. This way, they haven't."

"All right, gentlemen," I said, "I take it that we're agreed that we must all follow a single line of policy and not work at cross-purposes to each other?"

They all agreed to that instantly, but with a questioning note in their voices.

"Well, then, I trust you all realize that we cannot, under any circumstances, allow those three brothers to be convicted in this court," I added.

There was a moment of startled silence, while Hoddy and Stonehenge and Parros and Thrombley were understanding what they had just heard. Then Stonehenge cleared his throat and said:

"Mr. Ambassador! I'm sure that you have some excellent reasons for that remarkable statement, but I must say—"

"It was a really colossal error on somebody's part," I said, "that this case was allowed to get into the Court of Political Justice. It never should have. And if we take a part in the prosecution, or allow those men to be convicted, we will establish a precedent to support the principle that a foreign Ambassador is, on this planet, defined as a practicing local politician.

"I will invite you to digest that for a moment."

A moment was all they needed. Thrombley was horrified and dithered incoherently. Stonehenge frowned and fidgeted with some papers in front of him. I could see several thoughts gathering behind his eyes, including, I was sure, a new view of his instructions from Klüng.

Even Hoddy got at least part of it. "Why, that means that anybody can bump off any diplomat he doesn't like…" he began.

"That is only part of it, Mr. Ringo," Thrombley told him. "It also means that a diplomat, instead of being regarded as the representative of his own government, becomes, in effect, a functionary of the government of New Texas. Why, all sorts of complications could arise…"

"It certainly would impair, shall we say, the principle of extraterritoriality of Embassies," Stonehenge picked it up. "And it would practically destroy the principle of diplomatic immunity."

"Migawd!" Hoddy looked around nervously, as though he could already hear an army of New Texas Rangers, each with a warrant for Hoddy Ringo, battering at the gates.

"We'll have to do something!" Gomez, the Secretary of the Embassy, said.

"I don't know what," Stonehenge said. "The obvious solution would be, of course, to bring charges against those Bonney Boys on simple first-degree murder, which would be tried in an ordinary criminal court. But it's too late for that now. We wouldn't have time to prevent their being arraigned in this Political Justice court, and once a defendant is brought into court, on this planet, he cannot be brought into court again for the same act. Not the same *crime*, the same *act*."

I had been thinking about this and I was ready. "Look, we must bring those Bonney brothers to trial. It's the only effective way of demonstrating to the public the simple fact that Ambassador Cumshaw was murdered at the instigation of the z'Srauff. We dare not allow them to be convicted in the Court of Political Justice, for the reasons already stated. And to maintain the prestige of the Solar League, we dare not allow them to go unpunished."

"We can have it one way," Parros said, "and maybe we can have it two ways. But I'm damned if I can see how we can have it all three ways."

I wasn't surprised that he didn't see it; he hadn't had the same urgency goading him which had forced me to find the answer. It wasn't an answer that I liked, but I was in the position where I had no choice.

"Well, here's what we have to do, gentlemen," I began, and from the respectful way they regarded me, from the attention they were giving my words, I got a sudden thrill of pride. For the first time since my scrambled arrival, I was really *Ambassador* Stephen Silk.

CHAPTER EIGHT

A couple of New Texas Ranger tanks met the Embassy car four blocks from the Statehouse and convoyed us into the central plaza, where the barbecue had been held on the Friday afternoon that I had arrived on New Texas. There was almost as dense a crowd as the last time I had seen the place; but they were quieter, to the extent that there were no bands, and no shooting, no cowbells or whistles. The barbecue pits were going again, however, and hawkers were pushing or propelling their little wagons about, vending sandwiches. I saw a half a dozen big twenty-foot teleview screens, apparently wired from the courtroom.

As soon as the Embassy car and its escorting tanks reached the plaza, an ovation broke out. I was cheered, with the high-pitched *yipeee!* of New Texans and adjured and implored not to let them so-and-sos get away with it.

There was a veritable army of Rangers on guard at the doors of the courtroom. The only spectators being admitted to the courtroom seemed to be prominent citizens with enough pull to secure passes.

Inside, some of the spectators' benches had been removed to clear the front of the room. In the cleared space, there was one bulky shape under a cloth cover that seemed to be the air-car and another cloth-covered shape that looked like a fifty-mm dual-purpose gun. Smaller exhibits, including a twenty-mm auto-rifle, were piled on the friends-of-the-court table. The prosecution table was already occupied—Colonel Hickock, who waved a greeting to me, three or four men who looked like well-to-do ranchers, and a delegation of lawyers.

"Samuel Goodham," Parros, beside me, whispered, indicating a big, heavy-set man with white hair, dressed in a dark suit of the cut that had been fashionable on Terra seventy-five years ago. "Best criminal lawyer on the planet. Hickock must have hired him."

There was quite a swarm at the center table, too. Some of them were ranchers, a couple in aggressively shabby workclothes, and there were several members of the Diplomatic Corps. I shook hands with them and gathered that they, like myself, were worried about the precedent that might be established by this trial. While I was introducing Hoddy Ringo as my attaché extraordinary, which was no less than the truth, the defense party came in.

There were only three lawyers—a little, rodent-faced fellow, whom Parros pointed out as Clement Sidney, and two assistants. And, guarded by a Ranger and a couple of court-bailiffs, the three defendants, Switchblade Joe, Jack-High Abe and Turkey-Buzzard Tom Bonney. There was probably a year or so age different from one to another, but they certainly had a common parentage. They all had pale eyes and narrow, loose-lipped faces. Subnormal and probably psychopathic, I thought. Jack-High Abe had his left arm in a sling and his left shoulder in a plaster cast. The buzz of conversation among the spectators altered its tone subtly and took on a note of hostility as they entered and seated themselves.

The balcony seemed to be crowded with press representatives. Several telecast cameras and sound pickups had been rigged to cover the front of the room from various angles, a feature that had been missing from the trial I had seen with Gail on Friday.

Then the judges entered from a door behind the bench, which must have opened from a passageway under the plaza, and the court was called to order.

The President Judge was the same Nelson who had presided at the Whately trial and the first thing on the agenda seemed to be the selection of a new board of associate judges. Parros explained in a whisper that the board which had served on the previous trial would sit until that could be done.

A slip of paper was drawn from a box and a name was called. A man sitting on one of the front rows of spectators' seats got up and came forward. One of Sidney's assistants rummaged through a card file he had in front of him and handed a card to the chief of the defense. At once, Sidney was on his feet.

"Challenged, for cause!" he called out. "This man is known to have declared, in conversation at the bar of the Silver Peso Saloon, here in New Austin, that these three boys, my clients, ought all to be hanged higher than Haman."

"Yes, I said that!" the venireman declared. "I'll repeat it right here: all three of these murdering skunks ought to be hanged higher than—"

"Your Honor!" Sidney almost screamed. "If, after hearing this man's brazen declaration of bigoted class hatred against my clients, he is allowed to sit on that bench—"

Judge Nelson pounded with his gavel. "You don't have to instruct me in my judicial duties, Counselor," he said. "The venireman has obviously disqualified himself by giving evidence of prejudice. Next name."

The next man was challenged: he was a retired packing-house operator in New Austin, and had once expressed the opinion that Bonneyville and everybody in it ought to be H-bombed off the face of New Texas.

This Sidney seemed to have gotten the name of everybody likely to be called for court duty and had something on each one of them, because he went on like that all morning.

"You know what I think," Stonehenge whispered to me, leaning over behind Parros. "I think he's just stalling to keep the court in session until the z'Srauff fleet gets here. I wish we could get hold of one of those wrist watches."

"I can get you one, before evening," Hoddy offered, "if you don't care what happens to the mutt that's wearin' it."

"Better not," I decided. "Might tip them off to what we suspect. And we don't really need one: Sir Rodney will have patrols out far enough to get warning in time."

WE TOOK an hour, at noon, for lunch, and then it began again. By 1647, fifteen minutes before court should be adjourned, Judge Nelson ordered the bailiff to turn the clock back to 1300. The clock was turned back again when it reached 1645. By this time, Clement Sidney was probably the most unpopular man on New Texas.

Finally, Colonel Andrew J. Hickock rose to his feet.

"Your Honor: the present court is not obliged to retire from the bench until another court has been chosen as they are now sitting as a court in being. I propose that the trial begin, with the present court on the bench."

Sidney began yelling protests. Hoddy Ringo pulled his neckerchief around under his left ear and held the ends above his head. Nanadabadian, the Ambassador from Beta

Cephus IV, drew his biggest knife and began trying the edge on a sheet of paper.

"Well, Your Honor, I certainly do not wish to act in an obstructionist manner. The defense agrees to accept the present court," Sidney decided.

"Prosecution agrees to accept the present court," Goodham parroted.

"The present court will continue on the bench, to try the case of the Friends of Silas Cumshaw, deceased, versus Switchblade Joe Bonney, Jack-High Abe Bonney, Turkey-Buzzard Tom Bonney, et als." Judge Nelson rapped with his gavel. "Court is herewith adjourned until 0900 tomorrow."

The trial got started the next morning with a minimum amount of objections from Sidney. The charges and specifications were duly read, the three defendants pleaded not guilty, and then Goodham advanced with a paper in his hand to address the court. Sidney scampered up to take his position beside him.

"Your Honor, the prosecution wishes, subject to agreement of the defense, to enter the following stipulations, to wit: First, that the late Silas Cumshaw was a practicing politician within the meaning of the law. Second, that he is now dead, and came to his death in the manner attested to by the coroner of Sam Houston Continent. Third, that he came to his death at the hands of the defendants here present."

In all my planning, I'd forgotten that. I couldn't let those stipulations stand without protest, and at the same time, if I protested the characterization of Cumshaw as a practicing politician, the trial could easily end right there. So I prayed for a miracle, and Clement Sidney promptly obliged me.

"Defense won't stipulate anything!" he barked. "My clients, here, are victims of a monstrous conspiracy, a conspiracy to conceal the true facts of the death of Silas Cumshaw. They ought never to have been arrested or brought here, and if the prosecution wants to establish anything, they can do it by testimony, in the regular and lawful way. This practice of free-wheeling stipulation is only one of the many devices by which the courts of this planet are being perverted to serve the corrupt and unjust ends of a gang of reactionary landowners!"

Judge Nelson's gavel hit the bench with a crack like a rifle shot.

"Mr. Sidney! In justice to your clients, I would hate to force them to change lawyers in the middle of their trial, but if I hear another remark like that about the courts of New Texas, that's exactly what will happen, because you'll be in jail for contempt! Is that clear, Mr. Sidney?"

I settled back with a deep sigh of relief which got me, I noticed, curious stares from my fellow Ambassadors. I disregarded the questions in their glances; I had what I wanted.

They began calling up the witnesses.

First, the doctor who had certified Ambassador Cumshaw's death. He gave a concise description of the wounds which had killed my predecessor. Sidney was trying to make something out of the fact that he was Hickock's family physician, and consuming more time, when I got up.

"Your Honor, I am present here as *amicus curiae*, because of the obvious interest which the Government of the Solar League has in this case…"

"Objection!" Sidney yelled.

"Please state it," Nelson invited.

"This is a court of the people of the planet of New Texas. This foreign emissary of the Solar League, sent here to conspire with New Texan traitors to the end that New Texans shall be reduced to a supine and ravished satrapy of the all-devouring empire of the Galaxy—"

Judge Nelson rapped sharply.

"Friends of the court are defined as persons having a proper interest in the case. As this case arises from the death of the former Ambassador of the Solar League, I cannot see how the present Ambassador and his staff can be excluded. Overruled." He nodded to me. "Continue, Mr. Ambassador."

"As I understand, I have the same rights of cross-examination of witnesses as counsel for the prosecution and defense; is that correct, Your Honor?" It was, so I turned to the witness. "I suppose, Doctor, that you have had quite a bit of experience, in your practice, with gunshot wounds?"

He chuckled. "Mr. Ambassador, it is gunshot-wound cases which keep the practice of medicine and surgery alive on this planet. Yes, I definitely have."

"Now, you say that the deceased was hit by six different projectiles: right shoulder almost completely severed, right lung and right ribs blown out of the chest, spleen and kidneys so intermingled as to be practically one, and left leg severed by complete shattering of the left pelvis and hip-joint?"

"That's right."

I picked up the 20-mm auto-rifle—it weighed a good sixty pounds—from the table, and asked him if this weapon could have inflicted such wounds. He agreed that it both could and had.

"This the usual type of weapon used in your New Texas political liquidations?" I asked.

"Certainly not. The usual weapons are pistols; sometimes a hunting-rifle or a shotgun."

I asked the same question when I cross-examined the ballistics witness.

"Is this the usual type of weapon used in your New Texas political liquidations?"

"No, not at all. That's a very expensive weapon, Mr. Ambassador. Wasn't even manufactured on this planet; made by the z'Srauff star-cluster. A weapon like that sells for five, six hundred pesos. It's used for shooting really big game—supermastodon, and things like that. And, of course, for combat."

"It seems," I remarked, "that the defense is overlooking an obvious point there. I doubt if these three defendants ever, in all their lives, had among them the price of such a weapon."

That, of course, brought Sidney to his feet, sputtering objections to this attempt to disparage the honest poverty of his clients, which only helped to call attention to the point.

Then the prosecution called in a witness named David Crockett Longfellow. I'd met him at the Hickock ranch; he was Hickock's butler. He limped from an old injury which had retired him from work on the range. He was sworn in and testified to his name and occupation.

"Do you know these three defendants?" Goodham asked him.

"Yeah. I even marked one of them for future identification," Longfellow replied.

Sidney was up at once, shouting objections. After he was quieted down, Goodham remarked that he'd come to that point later, and began a line of questioning to establish that Longfellow had been on the Hickock ranch on the day when Silas Cumshaw was killed.

"Now," Goodham said, "will you relate to the court the matters of interest which came to your personal observation on that day."

Longfellow began his story. "At about 0900, I was dustin' up and straightenin' things in the library while the Colonel was at his desk. All of a sudden, he said to me, 'Davy, suppose you call the Solar Embassy and see if Mr. Cumshaw is doin' anything today; if he isn't, ask him if he wants to come out.' I was workin' right beside the telescreen. So I called the Solar League Embassy. Mr. Thrombley took the call, and I asked him was Mr. Cumshaw around. By this time, the Colonel got through with what he was doin' at the desk and came over to the screen. I went back to my work, but I heard the Colonel askin' Mr. Cumshaw could he come out for the day, an' Mr. Cumshaw sayin', yes, he could; he'd be out by about 1030.

"Well, 'long about 1030, his air-car came in and landed on the drive. Little single-seat job that he drove himself. He landed it about a hundred feet from the outside veranda, like he usually did, and got out.

"Then, this other car came droppin' in from outa nowhere. I didn't pay it much attention; thought it might be one of the other Ambassadors that Mr. Cumshaw'd brung along. But Mr. Cumshaw turned around and looked at it, and then he started to run for the veranda. I was standin' in the doorway when I seen him startin' to run. I jumped out on the porch, quick-like, and pulled my gun, and then this auto-rifle begun firin' outa the other car. There was only eight or ten shots fired from this car, but most of them hit Mr. Cumshaw."

Goodham waited a few moments. Longfellow's voice had choked and there was a twitching about his face, as though he were trying to suppress tears.

"Now, Mr. Longfellow," Goodham said, "did you recognize the people who were in the car from which the shots came?"

"Yeah. Like I said, I cut a mark on one of them. That one there: Jack-High Abe Bonney. He was handlin' the gun, and from where I was, he had his left side to me. I was tryin' for his head, but I always overshoot, so I have the habit of holdin' low. This time I held too low." He looked at Jack-High in coldly poisonous hatred. "I'll be sorry about that as long as I live."

"And who else was in the car?"

"The other two curs outa the same litter: Switchblade an' Turkey-Buzzard, over there."

Further questioning revealed that Longfellow had had no direct knowledge of the pursuit, or the siege of the jail in Bonneyville. Colonel Hickock had taken personal command of that, and had left Longfellow behind to call the Solar League Embassy and the Rangers. He had made no attempt to move the body, but had left it lying in the driveway until the doctor and the Rangers arrived.

Goodham went to the middle table and picked up a heavy automatic pistol.

"I call the court's attention to this pistol. It is an eleven-mm automatic, manufactured by the Colt Firearms Company of New Texas, a licensed subsidiary of the Colt Firearms Company of Terra." He handed it to Longfellow. "Do you know this pistol?" he asked.

Longfellow was almost insulted by the question. Of course he knew his own pistol. He recited the serial number, and pointed to different scars and scratches on the weapon, telling how they had been acquired.

"The court accepts that Mr. Longfellow knows his own weapon," Nelson said. "I assume that this is the weapon with which you claim to have shot Jack-High Abe Bonney?"

It was, although Longfellow resented the qualification.

"That's all. Your witness, Mr. Sidney," Goodham said.

Sidney began an immediate attack.

Questioning Longfellow's eyesight, intelligence, honesty and integrity, he tried to show personal enmity toward the Bonneys. He implied that Longfellow had been conspiring with Cumshaw to bring about the conquest of New Texas by the Solar League. The verbal exchange became so heated that both witness and attorney had to be admonished repeatedly from the bench. But at no point did Sidney shake Longfellow from his one fundamental statement, that the Bonney brothers had shot Silas Cumshaw and that he had shot Jack-High Abe Bonney in the shoulder.

When he was finished, I got up and took over.

"Mr. Longfellow, you say that Mr. Thrombley answered the screen at the Solar League Embassy," I began. "You know Mr. Thrombley?"

"Sure, Mr. Silk. He's been out at the ranch with Mr. Cumshaw a lotta times."

"Well, beside yourself and Colonel Hickock and Mr. Cumshaw and, possibly, Mr. Thrombley, who else knew that Mr. Cumshaw would be at the ranch at 1030 on that morning?"

Nobody. But the aircar had obviously been waiting for Mr. Cumshaw; the Bonneys must have had advance knowledge. My questions made that point clear despite the obvious—and reluctantly court-sustained—objections from Mr. Sidney.

"That will be all, Mr. Longfellow; thank you. Any questions from anybody else?"

There being none, Longfellow stepped down. It was then a few minutes before noon, so Judge Nelson recessed court for an hour and a half.

IN THE afternoon, the surgeon who had treated Jack-High Abe Bonney's wounded shoulder testified at great length, identifying the bullet that had been extracted out of Bonney's shoulder. A ballistics man from Ranger crime-lab followed him to the stand and testified that it had been fired from Longfellow's Colt. After that Ranger Captain Nelson rose and took the stand. His testimony was about what he had given me at the Embassy, with the exception that the Bonneys' admission that they had shot Ambassador Cumshaw was ruled out as having been made under duress.

However, Captain Nelson's testimony didn't need the confessions.

The cover was stripped off the air-car, and a couple of men with a power-dolly dragged it out in front of the bench. The Ranger Captain identified it as the car that he had found at the Bonneyville jail. He went over it with an ultra-violet flashlight and showed where he had written his name and the date on it with fluorescent ink. The effects of AA-fire were plainly evident on it.

Then the other shrouded object was unveiled and identified as the gun which had disabled the air-car. Colonel Hickock identified the gun as the one with which he had fired on the air-car. Finally, the ballistics expert was brought back to the stand again, to link the two by means of fragments found in the car.

Then Goodham brought Kettle-Belly Sam Bonney to the stand.

The Mayor of Bonneyville was a man of fifty or so, short, partially bald, dressed in faded blue Levis, a frayed white shirt, and a grease-spotted vest. There was absolutely no mystery about how he had acquired his nickname. He disgorged a cud of tobacco into a spittoon, took the oath with unctuous solemnity, then reloaded himself with another chew and told his version of the attack on the jail.

Somewhere around 10:45 on the specific day in question, he testified, he had been in his office, hard at work in the public service, when an air-car, partially disabled by gunfire, had landed in the street outside and the three defendants had rushed in, claiming sanctuary. From that point on, the story flowed along smoothly, following the lines predicted by Captain Nelson and Parros. Of course he had given the fugitives shelter; they had claimed to have been near to a political assassination and were in fear of their lives.

Under Sidney's cross-examination, and coaching, he poured out the story of Bonneyville's wrongs at the hands of the reactionary landowners, and the atrocious behavior of the Hickock goon-gang. Finally, after extracting the last drop of class-hatred venom out of him, Sidney turned him over to me.

"Just how many men were inside the jail facility when the three defendants had come in and claimed sanctuary?" I asked.

He couldn't rightly say, maybe four or five.

"Closer twenty-five, according to the Rangers. How many of them were prisoners in the jail?"

"Well, none. The prisoners was all turned out that mornin'. They was just common drunks, disorderly conduct cases, that kinda thing. We turned them out so's we could make some repairs."

"You turned them out because you expected to have to defend the jail; because you knew in advance that these three would be along claiming sanctuary, and that Colonel Hickock's ranch hands would be right on their heels, didn't you?" I demanded.

It took a good five minutes before Sidney stopped shouting long enough for Judge Nelson to sustain the objection.

"You knew these young men all their lives, I take it. What did you know about their financial circumstances, for instance?"

"Well, they've been ground down an' kept poor by the big ranchers an' the money-guys..."

"Then weren't you surprised to see them driving such an expensive aircar?"

"I don't know as it's such an expensive—" he shut his mouth suddenly.

"You know where they got the money to buy that car?" I pressed.

Kettle-Belly Sam didn't answer.

"From the man who paid them to murder Ambassador Silas Cumshaw?" I kept pressing. "Do you know how much they were paid for doing that job? Do you know the source of where the money came from? Do you know who the go-between was, and how much he got, and how much he kept for himself? Was it the same source that paid for the recent attempt on President Hutchinson's life?"

"I refuse to answer the question!" the witness loudly declared, trying to shove his chest out about half as far as his midriff. "On the grounds that it might incriminate or degrade me!"

"You can't degrade a Bonney!" a voice from the balcony put in.

"So then," I replied to the voice, "what he means is, incriminate." I turned to the witness. "That will be all. Excused."

As Bonney left the stand and was led out the side door, Goodham addressed the bench.

"Now, Your Honor," he said, "I believe that the prosecution has succeeded in definitely establishing that these three defendants actually did fire the shot which, on April 22, 2193, deprived Silas Cumshaw of his life. We will now undertake to prove…"

Followed a long succession of witnesses, each testifying to some public or private act of philanthropy, some noble trait of character. It was the sort of thing that the defense lawyer in the Whately case had been so willing to stipulate. Sidney, of course, tried to make it all out to be part of a sinister conspiracy to help establish a Solar League fifth column on New Texas. Finally, the prosecution rested its case.

I entertained Gail and her father for a while at the Embassy that evening. The street outside the building was crowded with a large group of New Texans, virtually all of them on our side, loudly shouting slogans like, "Death to the Bonneys!" and "Vengeance for Cumshaw!" and "Annexation Now!" Some of it was entirely spontaneous, too. The Hickocks, father and daughter, were given a tremendous ovation, when they finally left, and followed to their hotel by cheering crowds. I saw one big banner, lettered: 'DON'T LET NEW TEXAS GO TO THE DOGS.' and bearing a crude picture of a z'Srauff. I seemed to recall having seen a couple of our Marines making that banner the evening before in the Embassy patio, but…

CHAPTER TEN

The next morning, the third of the trial, opened with the defense witnesses, character-witnesses for the three killers and witnesses to the political iniquities of Silas Cumshaw.

Neither Goodham nor I bothered to cross-examine the former. I couldn't see how any lawyer as shrewd as Sidney had shown himself to be would even dream of getting such an array of thugs, cutthroats, sluts and slatterns into court as character witnesses for anybody.

The latter, on the other hand, we went after unmercifully, revealing, under their enmity for Cumshaw, a small, hard core of bigoted xenophobia and selfish fear. Goodham did a beautiful job on that; he seemed able, at a glance, to divine exactly what each witness's motivation was, and able to make him or her betray that motivation in its least admirable terms. Finally the defense rested, about a quarter-hour before noon.

I rose and addressed the court:

"Your Honor, while both the prosecution and the defense have done an admirable job in bringing out the essential facts of how my predecessor met his death, there are many features about this case which are far from clear to me. They will be even less clear to my government, which is composed of men who have never set foot on this planet. For this reason, I wish to call, or recall, certain witnesses to clarify these points."

Sidney, who had begun shouting objections as soon as I had gotten to my feet, finally managed to get himself recognized by the court.

"This Solar League Ambassador, Your Honor, is simply trying to use the courts of the Planet of New Texas as a sounding-board for his imperialistic government's propaganda..."

"You may reassure yourself, Mr. Sidney," Judge Nelson said. "This court will not allow itself to be improperly used, or improperly swayed, by the Ambassador of the Solar League. This court is interested only in determining the facts regarding the case before it. You may call your witnesses, Mr. Ambassador." He glanced at his watch. "Court will now recess for an hour and a half; can you have them here by 1330?"

I assured him I could after glancing across the room at Ranger Captain Nelson and catching his nod.

MY FIRST that afternoon was Thrombley. After the formalities of getting his name and connection with the Solar League Embassy on the record, I asked him, "Mr. Thrombley, did you, on the morning of April 22, receive a call from the Hickock ranch for Mr. Cumshaw?"

"Yes, indeed, Mr. Ambassador. The call was from Mr. Longfellow, Colonel Hickock's butler. He asked if Mr. Cumshaw were available. It happened that Mr. Cumshaw was in the same room with me, and he came directly to the screen. Then Colonel Hickock appeared in the screen, and inquired if Mr. Cumshaw could come out to the ranch for the day; he said something about superdove shooting."

"You heard Mr. Cumshaw tell Colonel Hickock that he would be out at the ranch at about 1030?" Thrombley said he had. "And, to your knowledge, did anybody else at the Embassy hear that?"

"Oh, no, sir; we were in the Ambassador's private office, and the screen there is tap-proof."

"And what other calls did you receive, prior to Mr. Cumshaw's death?"

"About fifteen minutes after Mr. Cumshaw had left, the z'Srauff Ambassador called, about a personal matter. As he was most anxious to contact Mr. Cumshaw, I told him where he had gone."

"Then, to your knowledge, outside of yourself, Colonel Hickock, and his butler, the z'Srauff Ambassador was the only person who could have known that Mr. Cumshaw's car would be landing on Colonel Hickock's drive at or about 1030. Is that correct?"

"Yes, plus anybody whom the z'Srauff Ambassador might have told."

"Exactly!" I pounced. Then I turned and gave the three Bonney brothers a sweeping glance. "Plus anybody the z'Srauff Ambassador might have told... That's all. Your witness, Mr. Sidney."

Sidney got up, started toward the witness stand, and then thought better of it.

"No questions," he said.

The next witness was a Mr. James Finnegan; he was identified as cashier of the Crooked Creek National Bank. I asked him if Kettle-Belly Sam Bonney did business at his bank; he said yes.

"Anything unusual about Mayor Bonney's account?" I asked.

"Well, it's been unusually active lately. Ordinarily, he carries around two-three thousand pesos, but about the first of April, that took a big jump. Quite a big jump; two hundred and fifty thousand pesos, all in a lump."

"When did Kettle-Belly Sam deposit this large sum?" I asked.

"He didn't. The money came to us in a cashier's check on the Ranchers' Trust Company of New Austin with an anonymous letter asking that it be deposited to Mayor Bonney's account. The letter was typed on a sheet of yellow paper in Basic English."

"Do you have that letter now?" I asked.

"No, I don't. After we'd recorded the new balance, Kettle-Belly came storming in, raising hell because we'd recorded it. He told me that if we ever got another deposit like that, we were to turn it over to him in cash. Then he wanted to see the letter, and when I gave it to him, he took it over to a telescreen booth, and drew the curtains. I got a little busy with some other matters, and the next time I looked, Kettle-Belly was gone and some girl was using the booth."

"That's very interesting, Mr. Finnegan. Was that the last of your unusual business with Mayor Bonney?"

"Oh, no. Then, about two weeks before Mr. Cumshaw was killed, Kettle-Belly came in and wanted 50,000 pesos, in a big hurry, in small bills. I gave it to him, and he grabbed at the money like a starved dog at a bone, and upset a bottle of red perma-ink, the sort we use to refill our bank seals. Three of the bills got splashed. I offered to exchange them, but he said, 'Hell with it; I'm in a hurry,' and went out. The next day, Switchblade Joe Bonney came in to make payment on a note we were holding on him. He used those three bills in the payment.

"Then, about a week ago, there was another cashier's check came in for Kettle-Belly. This time, there was no letter; just one of our regular deposit-slips. No name of depositor. I held the check, and gave it to Kettle-Belly. I remember, when it came in, I said to one of the clerks, 'Well, I wonder who's going to get bumped off this time.' And sure enough…"

Sidney's yell of, "Objection!" was all his previous objections gathered into one.

"You say the letter accompanying the first deposit, the one in Basic English, was apparently taken away by Kettle-Belly Sam Bonney. If you saw another letter of the same sort, would you be able to say whether or not it might be like the one you mentioned?"

Sidney vociferating more objections; I was trying to get expert testimony without previous qualification…

"Not at all, Mr. Sidney," Judge Nelson ruled. "Mr. Silk has merely asked if Mr. Finnegan could say whether one document bore any resemblance to another."

I asked permission to have another witness sworn in while Finnegan was still on the stand, and called in a Mr. Boone, the cashier of the Packers' and Brokers' Trust Company of New Austin. He had with him a letter, typed on yellow paper, which he said had accompanied an anonymous deposit of two hundred thousand pesos. Mr. Finnegan said that it was exactly like the one he had received, in typing, grammar and wording, all but the name of the person to whose account the money was to be deposited.

"And whose account received this anonymous benefaction, Mr. Boone?" I asked.

"The account," Boone replied, "of Mr. Clement Sidney."

I was surprised that Judge Nelson didn't break the handle of his gavel, after that. Finally, after a couple of threats to clear the court, order was restored. Mr. Sidney had no questions to ask this time, either.

The bailiff looked at the next slip of paper I gave him, frowned over it, and finally asked the court for assistance.

"I can't pronounce this-here thing, at all," he complained.

One of the judges finally got out a mouthful of growls and yaps, and gave it to the clerk of the court to copy into the record. The next witness was a z'Srauff, and in the New Texan garb he was wearing, he was something to open my eyes, even after years on the Hooligan Diplomats.

After he took the stand, the clerk of the court looked at him blankly for a moment. Then he turned to Judge Nelson.

"Your Honor, how am I gonna go about swearing him in?" he asked. "What does a z'Srauff swear by, that's binding?"

The President Judge frowned for a moment. "Does anybody here know Basic well enough to translate the oath?" he asked.

"I think I can," I offered. "I spent a great many years in our Consular Service, before I was sent here. We use Basic with a great many alien peoples."

"Administer the oath, then," Nelson told me.

"Put up right hand," I told the z'Srauff. "Do you truly say, in front of Great One who made all worlds, who has knowledge of what is in the hearts of all persons, that what you will say here will be true, all true, and not anything that is not true, and will you so say again at time when all worlds end? Do you so truly say?"

"Yes. I so truly say."

"Say your name."

"Ppmegll Kkuvtmmecc Cicici."

"What is your business?"

"I put things made of cloth into this world, and I take meat out of this world."

"Where do you have your house?"

"Here in New Austin, over my house of business, on Coronado Street."

"What people do you see in this place that you have made business with?"

Ppmegll Kkuvtmmecc Cicici pointed a three-fingered hand at the Bonney brothers.

"What business did you make with them?"

"I gave them for money a machine which goes on the ground and goes in the air very fast, to take persons and things about."

"Is that the thing you gave them for money?" I asked, pointing at the exhibit air-car.

"Yes, but it was new then. It has been made broken by things from guns now."

"What money did they give you for the machine?"

"One hundred pesos."

That started another uproar. There wasn't a soul in that courtroom who didn't know that five thousand pesos would have been a give-away bargain price for that car.

"Mr. Ambassador," one of the associate judges interrupted. "I used to be in the used-car business. Am I expected to believe that this…this being…sold that air-car for a hundred pesos?"

"Here's a notarized copy of the bill of sale, from the office of the Vehicles Registration Bureau," I said. "I introduce it as evidence."

There was a disturbance at the back of the room, and then the z'Srauff Ambassador, Gglafrr Ddespttann Vuvuvu, came stalking down the aisle, followed by a couple of Rangers and two of his attachés. He came forward and addressed the court.

"May you be happy, sir, but I am in here so quickly not because I have desire to make noise, but because it is only short time since it got in my knowledge that one of my persons is in this place. I am here to be of help to him that he not get in trouble, and to be of help to you. The name for what I am to do in this place is not part of my knowledge. Please say it for me."

"You are a friend of the court," Judge Nelson told him. "An *amicus curiae*."

"You make me happy. Please go on; I have no desire to put stop to what you do in this place."

"From what person did you get this machine that you gave to these persons for one hundred pesos?" I asked.

Gglafrr immediately began barking and snarling and yelping at my witness. The drygoods importer looked startled, and Judge Nelson banged with his gavel.

"That's enough of that! There'll be nothing spoken in this court but English, except through an interpreter!"

"Yow! I am sad that what I did was not right," the z'Srauff Ambassador replied contritely. "But my person here has not as part of his knowledge that you will make him say what may put him in trouble."

Nelson nodded in agreement.

"You are right: this person who is here has no need to make answer to any question if it may put him in trouble or make him seem less than he is."

"I will not make answer," the witness said.

"No further questions."

I turned to Goodham, and then to Sidney; they had no questions, either. I handed another slip of paper to the bailiff, and another z'Srauff, named Bbrarkk Jjoknyyegg Kekeke took the stand.

He put into this world things for small persons to make amusement with; he took out of this world meat and leather. He had his house of business in New Austin, and he pointed out the three Bonneys as persons in this place that he saw that he had seen before.

"And what business did you make with them?" I asked.

"I gave them for money a gun which sends out things of twenty-millimeters very fast, to make death or hurt come to men and animals and does destruction to machines and things."

"Is this the gun?" I showed it to him.

"It could be. The gun was made in my world; many guns like it are made there. I am certain that this is the very gun."

I had a notarized copy of a customs house bill in which the gun was described and specified by serial number. I introduced it as evidence.

"How much money did these three persons give you for this gun?" I asked.

"Five pesos."

"The customs appraisal on this gun is six hundred pesos," I mentioned.

Immediately, Ambassador Vuvuvu was on his feet. "My person here has not as part of his knowledge that he may put himself in trouble by what he says to answer these questions."

That put a stop to that. Bbrarkk Jjoknyyegg Kekeke immediately took refuge in refusal to answer on grounds of self-incrimination.

"That is all, Your Honor," I said, "And now," I continued, when the witness had left the stand, "I have something further to present to the court, speaking both as *amicus curiae* and as Ambassador of the Solar League. This court cannot convict the three men who are here on trial. These men should have never been brought to trial in this court: it has no jurisdiction over this case. This was a simple case of first-degree murder, by hired assassins, committed against the Ambassador of one government at the instigation of another, not an act of political protest within the meaning of New Texan law."

There was a brief silence; both the court and the spectators were stunned, and most stunned of all were the three Bonney brothers, who had been watching, fear-sick, while I had been putting a rope around their necks. The uproar from the rear of the courtroom gave Judge Nelson a needed minute or so to collect his thoughts. After he had gotten order restored, he turned to me, grim-faced.

"Ambassador Silk, will you please elaborate on the extraordinary statement you have just made," he invited, as though every word had sharp corners that were sticking in his throat.

"Gladly, Your Honor." My words, too, were gouging and scraping my throat as they came out; I could feel my knees getting absurdly weak, and my mouth tasted as though I had an old copper penny in it.

"As I understand it, the laws of New Texas do not extend their ordinary protection to persons engaged in the practice of politics. An act of personal injury against a politician is considered criminal only to the extent that the politician injured has not, by his public acts, deserved the degree of severity with which he has been injured, and the Court of Political Justice is established for the purpose of determining whether or not there has been such an excess of severity in the treatment meted out by the accused to the injured or deceased politician. This gives rise, of course, to some interesting practices; for instance, what is at law a trial of the accused is, in substance, a trial of his victim. But in any case tried in this court, the accused must be a person who has injured or killed a man who is definable as a practicing politician under the government of New Texas.

"Speaking for my government, I must deny that these men should have been tried in this court for the murder of Silas Cumshaw. To do otherwise would establish the principle and precedent that our Ambassador, or any other Ambassador here, is a practicing politician under—mark that well, Your Honor—under the laws and government of New Texas. This would not only make of any Ambassador a permissable target for any marksman who happened to disapprove of the policies of another government, but more serious, it would place the Ambassador and his government in a subordinate position relative to the government of New Texas. This the government of the Solar League simply cannot tolerate, for reasons which it would be insulting to the intelligence of this court to enumerate."

"Mr. Silk," Judge Nelson said gravely. "This court takes full cognizance of the force of your arguments. However, I'd like to know why you permitted this trial to run to this length before entering this objection. Surely you could have made clear the position of your government at the beginning of this trial."

"Your Honor," I said, "had I done so, these defendants would have been released, and the facts behind their crime would have never come to light. I grant that the important function of this court is to determine questions of relative guilt and innocence. We must not lose sight, however, of the fact that the primary function of any court is to determine the truth, and only by the process of the trial of these depraved murderers-for-hire could the real author of the crime be uncovered.

"This was important, both for the government of the Solar League and the government of New Texas. My government now knows who procured the death of Silas Cumshaw, and we will take appropriate action. The government of New Texas has now had spelled out, in letters anyone can read, the fact that this beautiful planet is in truth a *battleground*. Awareness of this may save New Texas from being the scene of a larger and more destructive battle. New Texas also knows who are its enemies, and who can be counted upon to stand as its friends."

"Yes, Mr. Silk. Mr. Vuvuvu, I haven't heard any comment from you... No comment? Well, we'll have to close the court, to consider this phase of the question."

The black screen slid up, for the second time during the trial. There was silence for a moment, and then the room became a bubbling pot of sound. At least six fights broke out among the spectators within three minutes; the Rangers and court bailiffs were busy restoring order.

Gail Hickock, who had been sitting on the front row of the spectators' seats, came running up while I was still receiving the congratulations of my fellow diplomats.

"Stephen! How *could* you?" she demanded. "You know what you've done? You've gotten those murdering snakes turned loose!"

Andrew Jackson Hickock left the prosecution table and approached.

"Mr. Silk! You've just secured the freedom of three men who murdered one of my best friends!"

"Colonel Hickock, I believe I knew Silas Cumshaw before you did. He was one of my instructors at Dumbarton Oaks, and I have always had the deepest respect and admiration for him. But he taught me one thing, which you seem to have forgotten since you expatriated yourself—that in the Diplomatic Service, personal feelings don't count. The only thing of importance is the advancement of the policies of the Solar League."

"Silas and I were attachés together, at the old Embassy at Drammool, on Altair II," Colonel Hickock said. What else he might have said was lost in the sudden exclamation as the black screen slid down. In front of Judge Nelson, I saw, there were three pistol-belts, and three pairs of automatics.

"Switchblade Joe Bonney, Jack-High Abe Bonney, Turkey-Buzzard Tom Bonney, together with your counsel, approach the court and hear the verdict," Judge Nelson said.

The three defendants and their lawyer rose. The Bonneys were swaggering and laughing, but for a lawyer whose clients had just emerged from the shadow of the gallows, Sidney was looking remarkably unhappy. He probably had imagination enough to see what would be waiting for him outside.

"It pains me inexpressibly," Judge Nelson said, "to inform you three that this court cannot convict you of the cowardly murder of that learned and honorable old man, Silas Cumshaw, nor can you be brought to trial in any other court on New Texas again for that dastardly crime. Here are your weapons, which must be returned to you. Sort them out yourselves, because I won't dirty my fingers on them. And may you regret and feel shame for your despicable act as long as you live, which I hope won't be more than a few hours."

With that, he used the end of his gavel to push the three belts off the bench and onto the floor at the Bonneys' feet. They stood laughing at him for a few moments, then stopped, picked the belts up, drew the pistols to check magazines and chambers, and then began slapping each others' backs and shouting jubilant congratulations at one another. Sidney's two assistants and some of his friends came up and began pumping Sidney's hands.

"There!" Gail flung at me. "Now look at your masterpiece! Why don't you go up and congratulate him, too?"

And with that, she slapped me across the face. It hurt like the devil; she was a lot stronger than I'd expected.

"In about two minutes," I told her, "you can apologize to me for that, or weep over my corpse. Right now, though, you'd better be getting behind something solid."

CHAPTER ELEVEN

I turned and stepped forward to confront the Bonneys, mentally thanking Gail. Up until she'd slapped me, I'd been weak-kneed and dry-mouthed with what I had to do. Now I was just plain angry, and I found that I was thinking a lot more clearly. Jack-High Bonney's wounded left shoulder, I knew, wouldn't keep him from using his gun hand, but his shoulder muscles would be stiff enough to slow his draw. I'd intended saving him until I'd dealt with his brothers. Now, I remembered how he'd gotten that wound in the first place: he'd been the one who'd used the auto-rifle, out at the Hickock ranch. So I changed my plans and moved him up to top priority.

"Hold it!" I yelled at them. "You've been cleared of killing a politician, but you still have killing a Solar League Ambassador to answer for. Now get your hands full of guns, if you don't want to die with them empty!"

The crowd of sympathizers and felicitators simply exploded away from the Bonney brothers. Out of the corner of my eye, I saw Sidney and a fat, blowsy woman with brass-colored hair as they both tried to dive under the friends-of-the-court table at the same place. The Bonney brothers simply stood and stared at me, for an instant, unbelievingly, as I got my thumbs on the release-studs of my belt. Judge Nelson's gavel was hammering, and he was shouting:

"Court–of–Political–Justice–Confederate–Continent–of–New–Texas–is–herewith–adjourned–reconvene–0900–tomorrow. *Hit the floor!*"

"Damn! He means it!" Switchblade Joe Bonney exclaimed.

Then they all reached for their guns. They were still reaching when I pressed the studs and the Krupp-Tattas popped up into my hands, and I swung up my right-hand gun and shot Jack-High through the head. After that, I just let my subconscious take over. I saw gun flames jump out at me from the Bonneys' weapons, and I felt my own pistols leap and writhe in my hands, but I don't believe I was aware of hearing the shots, not even from my own weapons. The whole thing probably lasted five seconds, but it seemed like twenty minutes to me. Then there was nobody shooting at me, and nobody for me to shoot at; the big room was silent, and I was aware that Judge Nelson and his eight associates were rising cautiously from behind the bench.

I holstered my left-hand gun, removed and replaced the magazine of the right-hand gun, then holstered it and reloaded the other one. Hoddy Ringo and Francisco Parros and Commander Stonehenge were on their feet, their pistols drawn, covering the spectators' seats. Colonel Hickock had also drawn a pistol and he was covering Sidney with it, occasionally moving the muzzle to the left to include the z'Srauff Ambassador and his two attachés.

By this time, Nelson and the other eight judges were in their seats, trying to look calm and judicial.

"Your Honor," I said, "I fully realize that no judge likes to have his court turned into a shooting gallery. I can assure you, however, that my action here was not the result of any lack of respect for this court. It was pure necessity.

Your Honor can see that: my government could not permit this crime against its Ambassador to pass unpunished."

Judge Nelson nodded solemnly. "Court was adjourned when this little incident happened, Mr. Silk," he said.

He leaned forward and looked to where the three Bonney brothers were making a mess of blood on the floor. "I trust that nobody will construe my unofficial and personal comments here as establishing any legal precedent, and I wouldn't like to see this sort of thing become customary...but...you did that all by yourself, with those little beanshooters...? Not bad, not bad at all, Mr. Silk."

I thanked him, then turned to the z'Srauff Ambassador. I didn't bother putting my remarks into Basic. He understood, as well as I did, what I was saying.

"Look, Fido," I told him, "my government is quite well aware of the source from which the orders for the murder of my predecessor came. These men I just killed were only the tools.

"We're going to get the brains behind them, if we have to send every warship we own into the z'Srauff star-cluster and devastate every planet in it. We don't let dogs snap at us. And when they do, we don't kick them, we shoot them!"

That, of course, was not exactly striped-pants diplomatic language. I wondered, for a moment, what Norman Gazarian, the protocol man, would think if he heard an Ambassador calling another Ambassador Fido.

But it seemed to be the kind of language that Mr. Vuvuvu understood. He skinned back his upper lip at me and began snarling and growling. Then he turned on his hind paws and padded angrily down the aisle away from the front of the courtroom.

The spectators around him and above him began barking, baying, yelping at him: "Tie a can to his tail!" "Git for home, Bruno!"

Then somebody yelled, "Hey, look! Even his wrist watch is blushing!"

That was perfectly true. Mr. Gglafrr Ddespttann Vuvuvu's watch-face, normally white, was now glowing a bright ruby-red.

I looked at Stonehenge and found him looking at me. It would be full dark in four or five hours; there ought to be something spectacular to see in the cloudless skies of Capella IV tonight.

Fleet Admiral Sir Rodney Tregaskis would see to that.

FROM REPORT
OF SPACE-COMMANDER STONEHENGE
TO SECRETARY OF AGGRESSION, KLUNG:

...*so the measures considered by yourself and Secretary of State Ghopal Singh and Security Coördinator Natalenko, as transmitted to me by Mr. Hoddy Ringo, were not, I am glad to say, needed. Ambassador Silk, alive, handled the thing much better than Ambassador Silk, dead, could possibly have.*

...*to confirm Sir Rodney Tregaskis' report from the tales of the few survivors, the z'Srauff attack came as the Ambassador had expected. They dropped out of hyperspace about seventy light-minutes outside the Capella system, apparently in complete ignorance of the presence of our fleet.*

...*have learned the entire fleet consisted of about three hundred spaceships and reports reaching here indicate that no more than twenty got back to z'Srauff Cluster.*

...naturally, the whole affair has had a profound influence, an influence to the benefit of the Solar League, on all shades of public opinion.

...as you properly assumed, Mr. Hoddy Ringo is no longer with us. When it became apparent that the Palme-Silk Annexation Treaty would be ratified here, Mr. Ringo immediately saw that his status of diplomatic immunity would automatically terminate. Accordingly, he left this system, embarking from New Austin for Alderbaran IX, mentioning, as he shook hands with me, something about a widow. By a curious coincidence, the richest branch bank in the city was held up by a lone bandit about half an hour before he boarded the space-ship...

FINAL MESSAGE OF THE LAST
SOLAR AMBASSADOR TO
NEW TEXAS
STEPHEN SILK

Copies of the Treaty of Annexation, duly ratified by the New Texas Legislature, herewith.

Please note that the guarantees of non-intervention in local political institutions are the very minimum which are acceptable to the people of New Texas. They are especially adamant that there will be no change in their peculiar methods of insuring that their elected and appointed public officials shall be responsible to the electorate.

DEPARTMENT ADDENDUM

After the ratification of the Palme-Silk treaty, Mr. Silk remained on New Texas, married the daughter of a local rancher there (see file on First Ambassador, Colonel Andrew Jackson Hickock) and is still active in politics on that planet, often in opposition to Solar League policies, which he seems to anticipate with an almost uncanny prescience.

Natalenko re-read the addendum, pursed his thick lips and sighed. There were so many ways he could be using Mr. Stephen Silk...

For example—he looked at the tri-di star-map, both usefully and beautifully decorating his walls—over there, where Hoddy Ringo had gone, near Alderbaran IX.

Those were twin planets, one apparently settled by the equivalent descendants of the Edwards and the other inhabited by the children of a Jukes-Kallikak union. Even the Solar League Ambassadors there had taken the viewpoints of the planets to whom they were accredited, instead of the all-embracing view which their training should have given them...

Curious problem...and, how would Stephen Silk have handled it?

The Security Coordinator scrawled a note comprehensible only to himself...

THE END

If you've enjoyed this book, you will not want to miss these terrific titles…

ARMCHAIR SCI-FI & HORROR DOUBLE NOVELS, $12.95 each

D-71 **THE DEEP END** by Gregory Luce
TO WATCH BY NIGHT by Robert Moore Williams

D-72 **SWORDSMAN OF LOST TERRA** by Poul Anderson
PLANET OF GHOSTS by David V. Reed

D-73 **MOON OF BATTLE** by J. J. Allerton
THE MUTANT WEAPON by Murray Leinster

D-74 **OLD SPACEMEN NEVER DIE!** John Jakes
RETURN TO EARTH by Bryan Berry

D-75 **THE THING FROM UNDERNEATH** by Milton Lesser
OPERATION INTERSTELLAR by George O. Smith

D-76 **THE BURNING WORLD** by Algis Budrys
FOREVER IS TOO LONG by Chester S. Geier

D-77 **THE COSMIC JUNKMAN** by Rog Phillips
THE ULTIMATE WEAPON by John W. Campbell

D-78 **THE TIES OF EARTH** by James H. Schmitz
CUE FOR QUIET by Thomas L. Sherred

D-79 **SECRET OF THE MARTIANS** by Paul W. Fairman
THE VARIABLE MAN by Philip K. Dick

D-80 **THE GREEN GIRL** by Jack Williamson
THE ROBOT PERIL by Don Wilcox

ARMCHAIR SCIENCE FICTION CLASSICS, $12.95 each

C-25 **THE STAR KINGS**
by Edmond Hamilton

C-26 **NOT IN SOLITUDE**
by Kenneth Gantz

C-32 **PROMETHEUS II**
by S. J. Byrne

ARMCHAIR SCI-FI & HORROR GEMS SERIES, $12.95 each

G-7 **SCIENCE FICTION GEMS, Vol. Seven**
Jack Sharkey and others

G-8 **HORROR GEMS, Vol. Eight**
Seabury Quinn and others